I worry about running out of shampoo. I worry about the factories that make nut-free candy and yet cannot guarantee that they're made in a nut-free environment. I worry that there are no air bags in school buses. I worry about robots rising up against humanity. I used to worry a lot about dying, but I suppose I can cross that off the list now. But thanks to my unhelpful guidance councillor, I now have to worry about worrying.

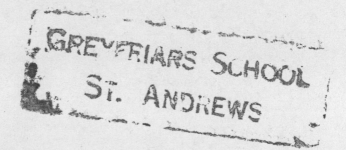

Metawars series

MEMOIRS OF A NEuROTIC ZOMBIE

JEFF NORTON

FABER & FABER

First published in 2014
by Faber and Faber Limited
Bloomsbury House,
74–77 Great Russell Street,
London, WC1B 3DA

Typeset by Faber and Faber
Printed in England by CPI Group (UK) Ltd, Croydon, CR0 4YY

A CIP record for this book
is available from the British Library

ISBN 978–0–571–30809–5

2 4 6 8 10 9 7 5 3

For Caden & Torin

Foreword

It has been an honour to be asked by Adam Meltzer to write his memoirs. I wrote this book from his notes and his recollections. I'm sure he would have written the book himself if he weren't so busy with school, comic books, and saving the world.

But the story is all his and I am merely the messenger.

Happy reading,

JEFF NORTON

P.S. You can get in touch with Adam at:
www.AdamMeltzer.com
or if you're old enough, through Facebook at:
www.facebook.com/AdamMeltzerZombie

Prologue
In Which I Introduce Myself

My name is Adam Meltzer. The last thing I remember was being stung by a bee while swinging at a robot-shaped piñata on my twelfth birthday. I was dead before the candy hit the ground.

That's right, I'm dead. But I'm alive . . . *ish*. The 'ish' is important. I'm the walking dead. *Talking* too. It's awkward and gross, and there's nothing anyone can do about it. You see, I died and then I came back . . . as a zombie.

Yep, there it is.

Zombie.

The big 'Z'.

It's a loaded word and makes most people think: brainless, cannibalistic monster. And if you think that too, then I hope these memoirs change your mind.

I still have a brain; I mean, how else would I be telling you all this? As for cannibalism, I have no interest in eating people. Even rare steak gives me indigestion and really bad gas. And my table manners are simply too good to accept the label of 'monster'.

I died, and now I'm back – zombified. Apparently there was a funeral, which I don't remember, and then a really dark grave, which I definitely do. It's hard to forget climbing up through two metres of dirt.

And I should tell you; I don't like dirt.

Or mess.

Or filth.

Of any kind.

The school guidance counsellor called it 'early onset' Obsessive Compulsive Disorder, but I say that when it comes to germs, it's better to catch them too early than too late. She also said I worry too much.

But I say: there's a *lot* to worry about.

I worry about running out of shampoo. I worry about the factories that make nut-free candy and yet cannot guarantee that they're made in a nut-free environment. I worry that there are no air bags in school buses. I worry about robots rising up against humanity. I used to worry a lot about dying, but I suppose I can cross that off the list now. But thanks to my unhelpful guidance counsellor, I now have to worry about worrying too much; so the list doesn't get any shorter.

This is my strange story, and I swear on a stack of vintage comic books that it's all true. So read on, if you dare.

But please wash your hands first. With antibac soap and hot water.

Ideally twice.

1

In Which I Get My Zombie On

I like to collect things. I started with stickers and stamps, and then graduated to comic books and travel-size soaps, shampoos and hand sanitizers. But my favourite collection is my range of drug pens.

My mom's a doctor and every week a parade of pharmaceutical* sales people come to her clinic to ask her to prescribe their brand-name (expensive) medicines instead of the generic (cheap) pills. They always give her little mementos like pens with the names of the drugs on them. And since Dr Mom only needs so many pens, she gives them to me.

I've collected two hundred and thirty-three drug pens, ranging from Aspirin to Zoloft. I have pens for depression, acne, high blood pressure, arthritis, and

---

* Pharmaceutical (pronounced: Farm-a-suit-ick-al): it's kind of a big, fancy word for medicine.

six for erectile dysfunction (that's an adult way of saying: wieners that don't work). My favourite pen is for a drug called Gastellex, which treats 'aggressive flatulence' (an adult way of saying: really bad farts) and it even makes a fart sound when you click it. You get all the funny fart sound without the actual smell or unseen poo particles spreading around the room. It's funny *and* hygienic! Win-win. I have pens for all sorts of ailments and diseases, but I don't have a pen for *death*.

In fact, there is no drug pen for death because (and yes, I have checked Wikipedia) there is currently no known treatment, therapy, ointment or cure for death. Hence, no pen.

People die and they don't come back. Death is the series finale of life, and there's no reunion show. It sucks, but it's true. And unless it happens to guys like Darth Vader's boss or Osama Bin Laden, it's pretty sad.

Death is a one-way street with no U-turns and no exceptions

But now there is an exception.

Me.

The *zombie*.

It's the best description for my condition. And not to be a stickler for detail – but once you're dead, there isn't a whole lot left to be a stickler for – I've decided to come to terms with the label. Sure, there are other words I could use: reanimated, walking dead, living dead, resurrected. But none of them feel quite *me*.

Reanimated sounds like I've been escaped from the Disney vault.

Walking Dead is that scary TV show, and I'm pretty sure it's a registered trademark.

Living Dead, well, that's literally a contradiction in terms.

Resurrected, maybe, but let's face it, that one's got a lot of Jesus connotations.

No, it's *zombie* all the way for me. I've been given a lot of labels in my twelve years of living – neurotic, sensitive, precocious, shower-hogger; and while I may still be all of those things, my new defining characteristic is probably that I'm technically dead.

I have no pulse, am legally deceased, and was even buried in a coffin that was very hard to climb out of. At this point, I should give Mom and Dad a major shout-out for not going all cinders and ashes on me. They cremated Gran when she died and then put her mortal remains in a ceramic urn. Thanks, guys, for not buying me a one-way ticket to Urnville!

So, instead of adorning the mantelpiece with Gran, I dug my way out of what I'd later learn was a very expensive coffin using my NinjaMan throwing-star belt buckle*. Of course, no one had thought to bury me with a set of house keys. When I finally made my way home, with the driest throat ever, I ding-donged the doorbell like I was trick-or-treating at my own house . . . and waited.

And waited.

It was a balmy Sunday morning. The gentiles were in church, Mom was in the back yard replanting her flower beds, and Dad was probably on the fourteenth hole.

Ding dong, I rang again.

Finally, the front door swung open and Mom just froze. She didn't scream. She didn't faint. She just stood there. I mean, she was probably expecting to be sold a box of Girl Guide cookies or sign a petition to put air bags in school buses, not to see her only son back from the dead – 100 per cent zombified.

---

* And thereby reducing its resale value on eBay.

Or, as I now like to say, *zomtastic*!

'Adam, is . . . it . . . you?' she stuttered, wiping the garden dirt on her jeans before reaching for a hug.

I put my arms up to hold her back. 'Oooh, Mom, maybe you should wash your hands properly,' I said. But because my mouth was so dry, what came out was: 'Aaargh Uuurgh Ooooh.'

'Is it for me?' called my sister from upstairs. She bounded down the steps and screamed.

Mom ignored her for once and stared at me. 'You're,' she said, searching for the word, 'alive?'

'OhMyGod!' gasped Amanda, a piece of cherry liquorice hanging from her quivering lips. 'What is *that?*'

But Mom kneeled down and enveloped me in a big bone-crusher of a hug. Seriously, she actually did crack a rib. It still smarts when I laugh or sneeze.

She reached for my hand, and led me inside. This time I froze. Mom's hands were filthy. But then I remembered I had grave dirt under my fingernails and decided not to judge.

'You're not letting it *in*, are you?' cried Amanda.

I limped to the kitchen, desperate for a glass of water, washed my hands (twice!) and helped myself to a bottle of water. I don't really do tap water because our urine and faeces go into the public water supply*. *Just saying.*

My rehydrated tongue finally allowed me to speak, so I asked the big question that was on my mind. 'When did we get new carpet in the hall?'

Okay, maybe that wasn't the *big* question, but it didn't escape my attention that I'd upset Mom by dumping dirt on the new plush. No wonder she was in tears. I was traipsing grave dirt everywhere and that carpet was not going to give up a stubborn stain easily. She looked really upset so I decided to change the subject from ruined floor coverings.

'Um, Mom, did I die?'

Mom blinked away her tears and slowly nodded her head, twirling her black curly hair like she always did when she was anxious. Amanda cowered in the corner brandishing a rolling pin.

'Is it really my little boy?' Mom sobbed.

---

* It's true, look it up. They chemically alter our pee before you drink it, and the poo gets scooped up and turned into giant poo cakes that are burned to make electricity. So, next time you charge your iPod, it could be powered by your own poo.

'I'm twelve,' I reminded her. 'I'm not a little boy!' It really irked me that they still treated me like the baby.

I'm only fifteen months younger than Amanda, and if you include death and unnatural resurrection, I've had waaaay more life and death experience than her. And yet she has a mobile phone and I don't. She has her own computer and I still have to share Mom's.

Amanda screwed up her freckled face. She was sporting red hair now, which was odd because yesterday I'd thought she was a blonde. 'Are you even human?' she asked from behind the rolling pin.

'Jeez, Amanda, what are you going to do, roll me into a pastry? And since when have you been a redhead?'

'It's Autumn Auburn,' she said.

'But it's *March*,' I reminded her.

'Oh, Adam,' cried my mother. 'It's . . . June.'

June?

Suddenly, nothing made sense. Where did the last three months go? And why would Amanda choose an autumnal hair dye for the start of the summer?

The world had gone mad.

I looked to Mom for answers even though she was clearly still upset about the carpet. But I needed to know. 'What happened to me?'

Of course, I had pretty much worked out the clawing-out-of-the-grave part for myself, but my memory was a *little* hazy about how I got there in the first place.

My mom took a big breath. 'Adam, you were stung by a bee and had a . . . terrible allergic reaction.'

But I wasn't allergic to bees.

I was allergic to shellfish, milk and milk by-products, the red dye used in hot dogs, and the rubber they make pencil erasers from. But not bees. I'd been tested for one hundred and twenty-seven potential allergens, including bee stingers both foreign and domestic and was given a clean bill of bee-health.

Nothing made sense.

Amanda puffed out her cheeks in mock swelling. 'I thought your head was going to explode,' she said.

'Amanda!' snapped my mom.

'By terrible,' I clarified, 'you mean *fatal*, right?'

'At your birthday party.' Mom started to sob again and gave me another hug. I braced myself for another cracked rib, but instead she just slumped on me. 'You collapsed and died from the reaction.'

With Mom blubbering, it didn't strike me as the right time to argue with her about her erroneous* diagnosis. I thought back to my birthday, which I suppose was also my *death*day, and it all came back to me:

The piñata, a Mexican party ritual popularised by Buy-Mart, was Mom's idea; probably to make little Ernesto, the shrimpy eleven year old who lives behind our house, feel a little less homesick. Nesto is actually third-generation American and the closest he's ever been to Mexico is the Taco Tavern on Main Street. But Mom's head is so filled with medical facts that she sometimes shortcuts to stereotypes.

It was unseasonably warm for March, and despite my protests that the early spring would bring disease-carrying mosquitos**, Mom insisted on holding the

---

* Erroneous means just plain wrong. I like it because it sounds like a dirty word, but really isn't.

** I was naturally concerned about West Nile Virus. We lived about 5,000 miles from the west bank of the River Nile, but those who think that distance will protect them from infection are in denial.

party outside. There were eight of us: me, puny Ernesto, the twins Tuck and Taylor Thompson (say that ten times fast!) from school, Jake O'Reilly who I buy comics with every Wednesday, Allen Doogle who always has the latest gaming console going (a good guy to know), and Kevin Krasowski who used to go to my school but moved to Dayton last year. Oh, and of course Amanda, who only attended because she had a crush on Kev's older brother and was hoping that he'd drive him down from Dayton. *He didn't.*

We formed a semi-circle around the helpless paper mâché robot hanging from the oak. The idea was to take turns whacking him with a stick until one of us cracked his shell and candy spilled out of his intestinal tract.

And you wonder why I worry about a robotic uprising!

As the birthday boy, it was my honour/duty to attack first. But as I held the stick for my first swing, something strange caught my eye. To be accurate, it wasn't a something, it was a some*one*. Two houses down, I spotted Corina Parker watching me from the window.

She stood perfectly still, half-shrouded in thick

curtain. She was pale and gaunt and dressed all in black (always in black), but didn't move. She just stared.

Our eyes met so I had to do something. I waved and she immediately ripped the curtain closed.

Nesto caught me gawking at her house and teased, 'Adam loves Corina!'

Everyone laughed at my idiot's grin and unreturned wave. Everyone but me, that is.

Now, for the record, I did not *love* Corina Parker. I hardly knew her. She moved to Croxton a year ago, and was in my class, but never once said 'Hi' to me (or to anyone as far as I could tell) and acts like she's so cool in her woe-is-me black garb. Her one-armed dad opened a successful dental practice in the mall where I've been for check-ups twice (with no cavities). Her mom, who I think is really homesick from somewhere in Europe, stays in the house with the curtains drawn. In fact, that day was the first time I'd ever seen them open.

'Adam loves Corina,' Nesto mocked. 'She's gonna hatch his babies!'

A word about Ernesto: he can be a right pest sometimes. I mean, he's not a bad kid; he's just immature. He's only eleven; what do you expect? At least he's still gullible enough to be talked into doing my yard work, so he does have his uses. But be forewarned:

Ernesto Ortega smells.

Ever since he moved in behind us four summers ago, he's always had this musty odour. The stink lives in his uncombed black hair and seeps out of his pores. And if you get too close to Ernesto, you might smell too. It's kind of contagious. And if you haven't guessed by now; I don't like contagion.

'She's way too cool for you, Adam,' laughed Allen.

'She just doesn't know what she's missing,' cheered my mom.

Jake undercut Mom's supportive, if embarrassing, endorsement. 'Oh, she totally does Mrs Meltzer. Corina's in our maths class, but she ignores him.'

'Then show her your big swing!' urged my dad, his camera phone covering his face.

I was mortified.

Everyone chanted, 'Big swing! Big swing!'

'Go on, smash that piñata,' Dad said. 'For the camera.'

I decided to take out my embarrassment on the

robot. I pulled back my arm, stick in hand and ready to strike. I was going to get that candy, and I didn't care if I had to disembowel a paper mâché automaton to get it. I heard the buzz of the bee before I saw it. As I made contact with the robot's groin, the biggest bumblebee I'd ever seen took aim at my cheek.

Killer bees: not just an internet rumour.

2

In Which I Learn to Live with It

The more I thought about my birth/deathday, the more I realised the vast unfairness of it all. Not only did I die, but I never even got a chance to eat my dairy-free NinjaMan cake . . .

. . . Amanda slapped the rolling pin into her palm, shaking me back to the present. 'You went down hard.'

'AmandaGenevieveMeltzer!' shouted my mom, pulling herself off me and wiping her eyes with her still garden-soil-covered hands. *Ick*. 'This is a second chance to be kind to your baby broth—'

'I'm not a baby!' I reminded them.

'Of course not, Adam.' She twirled her hair and exhaled. 'Amanda, I'm sorry for shouting at you; this is all happening very fast and is a bit overwhelming and—'

'I know,' I said, empathising with her trauma,

'we'll get a steam cleaner for the carpet and it'll
be—'

'Adam, I love you,' Mom interrupted. 'But don't
give a loom about the carpet, I care that you're . . .
that you *were* . . . dead.'

The word hung in the kitchen like the smell of
Amanda's boy-band-inspired perfume.

'So I've really been dead for three months?'

Mom glanced at the kitchen clock. 'Three months,
four days, and . . . twenty-two minutes.'

Now I was overwhelmed. I'd missed three season
finales, both Easter and Passover (one for Dad, one
for Mom), and one Spring/Summer IKEA catalogue.

'Did you keep my shows on TiVo?' I asked.

Her blank face revealed the terrible truth. I felt
betrayed, but I didn't feel . . . dead.

'I don't really feel dead. I mean, I'm a bit stiff and—'

'Adam, it's probably easier for me to show you,'
Mom suggested. 'Do you want to look in the mirror?'

'Not really.' I knew I wouldn't look my best; what
with the hardwood splinters in my hair, dirt all over
my face, and dried sweat from my great coffin escape.
But Mom put her arm around me and walked into
the hallway to the guest bathroom, stoically ignoring

the soiled carpet by the front door.

'He might break it,' said Amanda. She followed us, keeping back what she must've considered to be a minimum safe distance.

When I looked in the mirror, I suddenly understood why Amanda was holding the rolling pin.

I came face to face with my ghastly complexion.

Since Mom was a doctor, we'd had all sorts of conversations about what to expect from puberty. I was the best-prepared pre-teen for zits, pimples, whiteheads, blackheads, and patchy peach fuzz. But the boy in the mirror wasn't puberty personified, he was grotesquely zombified.

My flesh was grey, decomposing and flaking off. There was a five-centimetre skinless patch on my forehead where my white skull shone through like a crescent moon on a cloudy night. My eyes had lost their natural hazel sparkle and were now that trendy grey colour that paint stores called *urban slate*.

I was a monster.

I stared at the freak show in the mirror. I couldn't believe what was staring back. *Was that really me?* I wanted to stop, but I couldn't look away.

'It's not all bad,' offered my mom, stroking my hair

and pulling out a coffin splinter. 'Tell me one good thing about what you see?'

That was her little cheer-up game that she played whenever Amanda or I were feeling low. I tried to play along.

'Well,' I sighed, trying to ignore my skin. 'My hair actually looks better.'

Death had somehow smoothed out my most unruly curls. I'd tried all of the commercially available conditioners, and none of them had the juice to relax my curls the way three months of coffin confinement did. Of course, my dark brown bouffant was still covered in grave dirt so a shampoo-rinse-repeat was definitely in order.

She smiled. 'Adam, I need to call your father now. Please don't go anywhere.'

As if! I was covered in soil and wasn't going anywhere until I'd had a full scrub down and a triple-floss oral-hygiene intervention.

'Okay,' I said. 'I think I'll start with my teeth.' The thought of three months without flossing was sending shivers down my stiffened spine.

'Just grab a new toothbrush from the guest cabinet,' Mom called.

'The *guest* cabinet?'

My family had moved on. They'd deleted my TV shows, put down new carpet, and they'd thrown away my NinjaMan toothbrush. They never expected to see me again.

I unwrapped the white toothbrush, emblazoned with a cartoon of a one-armed dentist and the words, 'I only need one arm to make you smile!' The mint tingled on my decaying teeth, but I knew that tingling sensation meant it was working. Over the reassuring sound of bristles sweeping away three months of plaque, I heard Mom on the phone bringing Dad's golf game to an abrupt end.

'I don't care if you're a *million* under par, Michael,' Mom said, enunciating every word. 'Get back here. *Immediately*. Adam just walked through the door.'

Amanda gaped at me from the hallway; rolling pin in hand, and finally asked the one question that would come to annoy me most throughout my zombiedom: 'Did you go to Heaven?'

I ignored her question, and not just because I wanted to hear what Mom had to say to Dad, but because I didn't want to dignify it with a response. I mean, here I was, a medical miracle – a zombie brushing his teeth – and all my stupid sister could think about is whether I'd made it past St Peter or not.

'Mi-chael,' Mom said in an urgent whisper, 'our son has returned and he's a zombie.'

Hearing Mom use the word made it feel real. I was a zombie and I'd just have to live with it.

3

In Which I Get On with My Afterlife

The rest of the day, my *zom*day, flew by with surprising normality. I locked myself in the shower and gave myself a soapy scrub, skipping my regular exfoliation routine for obvious reasons. I purged every spec of grave dirt from my hair and conditioned twice. It felt great to be clean.

Later, Dad cooked my favourite dinner, meatball pizza. Amanda eventually put down the rolling pin and updated her Facebook status to: 'My brother is back and there's no way I'm giving up *my* room.'

Mom claimed not to care about the carpet, but I could tell it was eating away at her insides.

'We could go to Buy-Mart to pick out a steam cleaner together,' I suggested. 'Like old times.'

Those were good times.

'You're not going out looking all decomposed,

are you?' scoffed Amanda as she added slices of red liquorice to her pizza.

Dad was more supportive. Despite leaving four holes of golf unplayed, he seemed generally pleased to see me.

'We've got to plot your comeback,' he said, thumbing his hand on his latest self-help guru book called *Winner Take All* by Dr Anthony Brazen. 'You've got what Dr Brazen here calls a *strike-twice*, a killer second chance. The question is: how are you going to make the most of it?'

Not by reading those motivational books, I wanted to say.

'By going back to school,' added my mom. 'There's only a few weeks left in the semester and he's got a lot of cramming to do.'

'I've been crammed in a coffin for three months—'

'Yeah, no way is he going back to school,' declared Amanda with her mouth full. 'I'm finally at the cool table and *zom*-bro here will get me banished for sure. Gawd-wouldn't-Marina-Thompson-just-love-that.'

'That's actually worth coming back for,' I said with a smile.

'Your mother's right, Adam,' said Dad. 'You may

be technically dead, but you still need to be educated to make the most of yourself. How are the meatballs, by the way?'

'Ace, Dad. Thanks.'

'Atta boy,' he said, nodding proudly.

I wasn't sure about going back to school because I'd be three months behind everyone. But any concern about my *academic career* (Dad's words) evaporated when I went upstairs to the room formerly known as My Bedroom. Instead of being warmly greeted by my NinjaMan posters and alphabetical collection of travel-sized hand sanitizers, I stepped into an unholy shrine to Justin Bieber. And unless some movie studio boss had cast the Bieb as NinjaMan, someone had a lot of explaining to do.

'Where's all my stuff?' I gasped. 'Where's NinjaMan? Where's my SaniGel monument? Where are my drug pens?'

Mom and Dad shuffled awkwardly at the door. The late, great George Michael was right: *guilty feet ain't got no rhythm**.

'We're really sorry, Adam,' Dad said, fessing up.

---

* My bad, I thought he was dead. He isn't.

'Your death was very hard on Amanda and she said she'd feel closer to you if she moved into your room.'

'Is that right,' I said. 'My room with the two windows, a view of the street, and a bigger closet.'

Mom tried to appease me. 'Your pen collection is safely boxed up in the basement with your picture books.'

'*Comic* books,' I corrected her.

Amanda pushed past my parents to put herself between me and the rest of the room. The rolling pin was back. She was clearly prepared to defend her occupied territory.

'Now, Adam dear,' explained Mom, 'we thought it would help your sister with the grieving process and we honestly didn't think you'd mind.'

'This is me *minding*! Where are all my clothes?'

'I'm afraid I donated them to charity, kiddo,' stated my Dad. 'To help the needy.'

'But *I'm* needy,' I said. 'Look at me! I've been wearing the same suit for three months!'

'We can buy your clothes back tomorrow,' Mom offered. 'Or I can surprise you with new ones.'

The prospect of a new wardrobe did cheer me up a bit, but I was still in a state of justified outrage.

I peered into Amanda's old room. It had been transformed into a home gym. I shrugged in disbelief.

'I've decided to tackle my physique,' said my dad. 'Dr Brazen says fitness—'

Amanda coughed. 'Midlifecrisis.'

Dad flexed his pipe-cleaner biceps. 'See the difference?'

I couldn't.

'Adam, dear,' said my mom, 'we all grieve in our own ways.'

I rolled my grey eyes. 'That's a lovely sentiment and perfect for a sympathy card, but where am I supposed to sleep?'

'You can have the basement,' said Amanda.

'It's creepy down there,' I protested.

'You major in creepy now,' said Amanda.

'Not constructive, Amanda,' scolded Dad.

'Fine,' I relented.

I actually didn't mind the basement that much. I used to sneak down there sometimes when I couldn't sleep and curl up on the lumpy cot we got from Gran's house when we moved her into the old people's home.

Even though Lumpy Cot squeaked and will

probably contribute to spinal problems later in life, it was like a reliable friend who was always there for me in times of Meltzer-grade insomnia. There was always something soothing about lying on Lumpy Cot in darkness, comforted by the scent of fabric softener from the laundry room.

'It's just a temporary arrangement,' promised Mom, 'until we get this whole zombie thing sorted out. It's a bit awkward for us.'

'Awkward! For you?'

'Yeah, we have to look at you,' said Amanda.

'Go to your room, young lady!' barked Mom. Amanda waltzed into my old room and twirled.

'Insult to injury alert,' I said.

'Let her be,' said my dad. 'Your sister's actually very upset about this whole thing.'

She flashed me a smirk and stuck her tongue out. *Classy.*

I couldn't believe it. I was a walking corpse, and they were worried about upsetting the Bieber worshipper.

That night, I pulled out Lumpy Cot from the storage room and ran a load of washing to fill the basement with the sweet scent of Bounce goodness. I didn't have any PJs of my own (and no, I was not going to wear Amanda's Justin Bieber 'dreamgown'), so I stripped down to my undershirt and NinjaMan briefs, crawled into Lumpy Cot, contorted myself around the lumps, and fell asleep.

I don't think I dreamt while I was dead in the coffin, so my brain must've had a lot of catching up to do. I dreamed about wading in a pool of antibac soap, appearing in an issue of NinjaMan comics, and the day that Amanda's natural parents came to take her back.

I was in a deep sleep until three in the morning when I was awoken by the sound of kittens in a blender*.

---

* Legal notice: I have never placed kittens in a blender. It's just a turn of phrase, and while I don't like cats because they lick their own anuses, I would never knowingly place them into any small appliance.

4

In Which I Learn Something New About Ernesto

One horrific howling was coming from the back yard. I bolted upright, my bones creaking and cartilage complaining, and stared out the basement window that overlooked the lawn. I couldn't believe my dead eyes. It was my neighbour Ernesto Ortega, hunched over, ready to hurl. He was about to fertilise Mom's tulips with the contents of his stomach.

Normally the sight of vomit would keep me inside, behind locked doors, but I knew Mom was very sensitive about her flower beds – her 'islands of calm'. Ever since some neighbourhood dog had started trashing them, her soothing hobby had become a source of stress. I felt honour-bound to defend them.

I opened the back door, limped up the cement steps, and whisper-shouted, 'Nesto, please don't puke on the tulips.'

He looked up at me and screamed.

It was hardly a fair reaction. I should have been the one doing the screaming since he was the *real* monster.

Ernesto's arms and legs were half covered in scales with furry patches. He was sprouting a tail as long as his body. The peach-fuzz on his prepubescent cheeks was morphing into green scales. If I didn't have such a strong aversion to my own vomit, I would have retched all over my mom's islands of calm right then and there. But I held down my meatballs like a man and said:

'Yeah, yeah, yeah, I'm a zombie, but you, you're . . .'

What was he?

'You're turning into a . . .'

My first thought, given the full moon, was obviously *werewolf*, but Nesto looked more like a fusion of a lizard and an underfed gorilla.

'Chupacabra,' he sneezed.

'Bless you,' I said, retaining my manners; even though he didn't bother to cover his mouth with his claw.

'No, Chup-a-ca-bra,' Nesto enunciated, before letting out another painful screech as his face elongated. He sprouted two giant incisors like a scaly sabre-toothed tiger and foamed at the mouth.

'Wow, Nesto, you're definitely a candidate for braces.'

'Please don't tell anyone, Adam. It's embarrassing.'

'Hardly! I've been begging for braces to straighten out my—'

'Not the braces!' Nesto howled. '*This!*'

He convulsed again as his eyes swelled into black ping-pong balls. His face scaled over and he looked like Jake's pet iguana.

'See what I mean?' he hissed, burying his iguana head in his claws. 'I'm hideous.'

'Um, no, Nest, it's crazy cool,' I lied. 'You're like a werewolf, but not as wolfy.'

He shook his lizard head. 'I wish. Werewolves get their own movies. I'm just a disgusting . . . monster.'

'Nesto, you're talking to the one guy who knows exactly how you feel. I'm a living corpse. I get it.'

He smiled, his sharp, foam-covered teeth glistening in the moonlight. 'Yeah, you do look pretty rough.'

Nesto convulsed again, the force of his chupa-change making his body shudder and spasm. I was torn between propping up his self-esteem and protecting my mom's long-suffering flower beds.

For the past few years, Mom complained that every time she planted new flowers, some unknown animal would trounce them. Now it all made sense.

'You're the one who's been trashing the tulips?'

'Once I mutate, I can't help myself,' he said sheepishly, or well, technically, chupishly. 'It happens every full moon,' he said, looking to the sky.

I followed his gaze to the lunar source of his transmutation, and that's when I spotted her. Standing on the roof of her house, two doors down, was Corina Parker, the mysterious goth daughter of my one-armed dentist.

'That doesn't look very safe,' I said.

'Aha! I knew it. You *do* love her.' Nesto launched into a sing-songy tease, 'Adam loves Corina, Adam loves—'

'I told you before I don't even—'

And then she jumped.

5

In Which I Finally Get to Talk to Corina Parker

It felt like time stood still as Corina hovered in mid-air for one long, final moment before falling to her death.

I felt incredibly guilty for not acting on what our school guidance counsellor called 'the warning signs'. The all-black wardrobe, the fact that she never brought a lunch to school and avoided eye contact with everyone. I should've seen this coming.

Corina had clearly been crying out for help, and the most I ever did was pay Jake O'Reilly a week's worth of comics to swap seats in maths so I could sit one row closer to her. I'd never even had the guts to say, 'Hi, how do you do?' And now I never would because I'd ignored the warning signs.

But when Corina Parker leaped off her roof, time didn't stand still. And she didn't fall.

She floated.

Corina hovered in the night sky, silhouetted by the full moon. And then she flew straight towards us.

She actually *flew*.

It was incredible to watch, but I was flooded by conflicting emotions. Sure I was relieved that she wasn't going to smash into the ground and that I wouldn't have to make a police statement, but I was also gripped with envy.

She could *fly*!

'That's not fair,' I uttered.

Ernesto grunted, 'Huh?'

Flight was the one superpower I'd always wanted, and Corina Parker had it. I mean, not even NinjaMan could fly. And he was the best. But somehow my weirdo, goth, European neighbour could defy gravity.

'She's flying this way,' I said. 'Stand up straight.'

'Just great,' Ernesto sighed. 'I finally get to talk to her and I'm covered in scales.'

He had a point. He was not about to make a good first impression. And the scales were the least of his problems. But then again, I wasn't exactly ready for yearbook photos.

What if I totally grossed her out?

But when Corina touched down and looked

at me, she didn't even bat an elongated eyelash at my decomposing skin. It may not have been eye contact, but it was the closest I'd ever got to acknowledgement of my existence in an entire year. I shuffled nervously, realising I was almost naked. But she turned to Ernesto, now fully in monster-mode and still down on all fours.

'So, you're the one who's been keeping me awake?' she asked. 'Coffins aren't soundproof, you know.'

Nesto scratched at the grass and made a sound that I can only describe as a cross between a hiss and a growl.

'He's a bit sensitive about his . . . condition,' I said.

'He should be,' she said. 'What are you, his shrink?'

'No, I, um,' I stammered ineloquently. 'Hi, how do you do?'

'How do you *do*?' she repeated. 'Who says that? People in black and white movies?'

'Okay, just "Hi" then. I'm Adam Meltzer, from number 31.'

'No, you *used* to be Adam Meltzer. You appear to be dead now, so you no longer have any right, title or interest to your legal name. Trust me, I know a thing or two about being unnatural.'

Unnatural.

That's what we were. Three utterly unnatural Croxton kids.

'Lame briefs,' she scoffed. 'NinjaMan can't even fly.'

Ernesto snorted, which I think was chupa-speak for laughter. But I was too in awe of Corina's ability to fly to be concerned about the state of my undress.

'But you can,' I said, still amazed and still envious.

'Aren't you master of the obvious?' she quipped back.

'Are you a superhero?' I asked.

'I'm no more a superhero than you are a model for Nivea,' she said.

Ernesto snorted again. He clearly thought this was hilarious.

I touched my decaying cheek. 'That's not very nice,' I said.

She tilted her head and smiled with her black lipstick. 'I'm not a very nice person.'

'*If* you are a person,' said Nesto. His tail was darting back and forth. I couldn't tell if he was nervous or excited – maybe a bit of both.

'At least I'm not an animal,' she said. 'If that's

what you're implying, foam-face.'

Nesto wiped his mouth with a claw.

'Then what *are* you, exactly?' I asked.

'The long answer or the short answer?' she asked.

'Short,' said Nesto as I said, 'Long.'

'Ugh, this is boring me already. Look, the best translation is *vampire*,' she explained. 'Well, half vampire. From my mother's side.'

Ernesto and I looked at one another. We both had the same fight-or-flight reflex. We chose flight. I took a few steps back to avoid any bloodsucking. Nesto scuttled behind me for safety.

Corina shook her head and rolled her eyes. Her black hair was cut in a brutal bob, razor sharp along her porcelain jawline.

'Like I'd have any interest in a . . . What are you, *exactly?*'

'Chupacabra,' Ernesto sighed.

'Is it contagious?' she quipped. It was like she was reading my mind.

'No, it's a family thing. It's been in our bloodline for a long time.'

'Nesto, are your mom and dad chupa-parents?' I asked.

He shook his head. 'It skips every few generations, and only afflicts the men.'

'Boys,' corrected Corina.

'My great-grandfather was one, but I'm the first since him.' Nesto explained that his family had moved to Croxton from the country because every month in monster-mode he'd tunnel through the fields and chomp on grazing cows. The farmers were getting trigger-happy. 'Adam says I'm basically like a werewolf, only . . .'

Corina finished his sentence. 'Nowhere near as cool.'

'You see?' said Nesto, turning his lizard head to me.

'Anyway, what are you afraid of, leather-face?' she asked, looking too closely at my complexion. 'I doubt you even have any blood circulating any more. Have you checked your pulse lately?'

I hadn't. I put my two fingers to my neck. Aside from decrepit skin, I felt absolutely nothing.

'But vampires suck blood, don't they?' I asked. 'You do know that blood can transfer infectious diseases.' She may have been prickly, but I thought it was only polite to warn her about the dangers of her bodily fluid swapping lifestyle.

'I'm a vegan.'

'Oh, sorry,' said Ernesto.

'Do you even know what that means?' she asked.

'It's a woman thing,' he said to me.

Corina huffed. 'It means I don't eat meat, or eggs, or dairy, or anything that comes from an animal.'

'But your jacket is leather, which comes from animals,' I said.

'I make an exception for Prada*,' she said.

'What *do* you eat?' asked Ernesto.

'I pretty much survive on Pop Rocks,' she said.

'Me too,' said Ernesto. 'You know, when I'm not killing livestock, or munching on rodents, or ripping the heads off chickens.'

'You do know about bacteria, don't you, Nesto?' I asked. 'What you can't see can kill you.'

He shook his head and Corina laughed. 'You're kind of neurotic, aren't you, Zom-boy? You *do* know they have pills for that.'

'Yeah, I've got the pen.'

There was an awkward silence that could only

---

* I had to look that up later. Prada is this super-expensive Italian fashion label and made me wonder if dentistry was that well paid.

42

be created by three tweenage monsters sizing each other up. I looked at Ernesto and Corina and tried to focus the conversation on to an area of common interest*.

'I like Pop Rocks too. Have you got any on you?'

'Uh, yeah,' she said as she pulled a pouch of sugar rocks from her shiny, black leather jacket. She poured a few in my hand and tipped some into Ernesto's lizard jaw.

So there we were, in my back yard, bathed in moonlight; a neurotic zombie, a reluctant chupacabra, and a vegan vampire, all gargling the satisfying taste explosions of carbonated candy.

And I had a hunch we were going to be best friends.

* This was a technique outlined in one of my dad's guru books called *It's Not You, It's You!*

43

6

In Which I Go Back to School (Of My Own Free Will)

I woke up early on Monday and raided Amanda's make-up stash while she was showering. I liberally applied foundation and blusher, which I've seen her do a thousand times, and did my best to get that *'While I may look like a walking skeleton, I'm actually alive'* look the beauty industry pushes.

'What do you think?' I asked the family at breakfast.

'You look like a ventriloquist's doll*,' said Amanda.

'I'm really sorry, Adam,' said Mom. 'I didn't realise you were into SMOOCH, otherwise I would have bought you a ticket for Field of Screams.'

SMOOCH is this heavy metal rock band where four British guys wear crazy make-up, dress up in

---

* Ventriloquist's Doll: A puppet that supposedly 'talks' when its owner speaks without using his or her mouth. File under 'creepy'.

outlandish costumes, and scream so loudly that peoples' ears are known to bleed. My parents grew up listening to them, and for some reason, Amanda loves them too. I, however, was convinced they should be institutionalised . . . or deported.

'Field of Screams is on Friday and everyone's going,' taunted Amanda. ''Cept you, cos it's sold out. You snooze, you lose.'

'I wasn't exactly snoozing.'

'I'm sorry, Adam,' said Mom, draping her stethoscope around her neck. 'But the show is sold out.'

She took one last bite of toast, kissed my head, and headed for the door. She stopped, turned to look at my dad, and they both stuck their tongues out at one another and pumped their fists in the air with their index and pinky fingers extended like miniature bull's horns. It lasted only a moment, but it was long enough to put me off my breakfast.

I dumped the rest of my soggy cereal (NinjaMan Fight-O's) and placed my bowl in the dishwasher. The yellow 'rinse aid' light was flashing a warning.

'Tell me that's not been flashing for three months?' I asked, knowing that I was the only one in the house who actually cared about streak-free glassware.

'I don't know, kiddo,' said my dad, ignoring my dishwasher anxiety and looking looking closely at my made-up face. 'Have you considered a mask? Like your hero, NinjaMan – he wears a mask. Or perhaps a Venetian-festival look?'

'I think I look alive and well,' I declared. 'And I'm going to school today!'

'You have the ultimate doctor's note,' said Amanda. 'An undertaker's note! And you actually want to go?'

'Well I don't want to just sit around, text frenemies, and eat liquorice like you do when you pretend to be sick.'

'It's a woman thing!' she snapped, pushing away her chocolate cereal. 'Ugh, just don't talk to me at school.'

'Like I would.'

As I walked down the school hallway, a strange hush fell over the students as they parted for me; staring and whispering. Seventh grade was the middle grade of middle school, so I was used to being basically invisible. But everyone slowed down and stared at me as I strolled to my first class. I felt really exposed, walking through a cloud of gossip:

Is that Adam Meltzer?

I thought he died.

His hair looks better, smoother.

What's he doing back?

Is he into make-up now?

What's the big deal? I was just a kid back from the grave. Granted, a kid, with too much rouge on his cheeks.

Is that Amanda's little brother?

I hear he's been touring with SMOOCH.

Before death, I'd been an anonymous seventh grader, now I was part of the rumour mill. I wondered if this is how the popular kids felt all the time.

But I didn't have time to bask in my newfound fame because suddenly I was yanked into a classroom.

'What are you doing here, you moron?' asked Corina, closing the door of the empty history classroom. After Saturday night, I was hoping for a secret handshake, a spirited high five, or at the very least a polite nod.

'You just pulled me in here,' I said.

'No, duh, at *school*! And who did your make-up? You look like my grandmother on bingo night. Gawd,

47

you're not one of those SMOOCH-heads are you?'

'I didn't want to stay home and eat liquorice,' I said.

'What's that got to do with—'

'Never mind, it's a woman thing,' I said. 'Listen, I just wanted to come back to school, and thought I was looking a bit too pale.'

'Well now you look like a clown. And not in a good way.'

'There's a good way?' I wondered.

She rubbed my cheeks, smoothing out the make-up. 'You can come back from the dead, but you can't come back to school.'

'Why not? Isn't it the law?'

'The law is for the living. Once you're dead, you're off the school register. Do you know what that means?'

I shook my head. I didn't know.

'Don't move or your rouge will smear,' she said, holding my jaw straight. 'It means that the school doesn't receive any money for you. Follow?'

I shook my head. I wasn't following. I was focusing on the sensation of Corina's ice-cold hands on my face.

'I said, "don't move". Adam, you're an accounting anomaly*.'

'Wait. Am I moron or an anomaly?'

She stopped fixing my make-up and gave me a lesson in school funding. 'A student who shouldn't be here costs the school board money. That means an investigation. An investigation means the government, and the government will find freaks like us, lock us up, and experiment on us. Why do you think my family left Transylvania? We got discovered.'

'Oh,' I replied. 'I didn't think—'

'No, Adam, you didn't,' she said. 'And now that you're the walking dead, you've got to use what's left of your decomposed brain and be smarter than you ever thought possible. If they come to investigate, they'll find you. They'll find Ernesto. They'll find me. And they'll take us to Guantanamo Bay or Area 51. Places where they don't have Pop Rocks, Netflix or the Geneva Convention.'

---

* Anomaly: something weird, something strange. In *Star Trek*, it usually leads to destruction and guys in red shirts getting killed. And yes, a pre-teen zombie is most definitely an anomaly.

'Wow,' I said, 'you sound worried . . . like me.'

Corina scowled at me. 'You don't get it, do you? I'm different – you're different. And different scares people. It's threatening. It's un-American.'

She pointed to the posters on the classroom wall: the Mayflower, pilgrims, the first Thanksgiving and a bonfire.

'Do you know what we're learning about in here?'

'Ancient history,' I said.

'The Salem Witch Trials. When the pilgrims killed people for being different. They burned people at the stake because they were different; because they didn't understand them.'

'That was a long, long time ago. Before Wikipedia.'

'It's in your blood,' she shuddered. 'I can smell it.'

'Yeah, but it's not good to live a life in fear,' I said, quoting NinjaMan's inspirational outlook on life.

'Yeah-but-nothing,' she scoffed. 'Try saying that when you've had to pack up your coffin in the middle of the night, clear town, and live in the station wagon with your weirdo parents for weeks until you find a new place to blend in. And besides, you live in fear of biological organisms you can't even see. So don't lecture me about fear. And when you quote a comic-book character, get it right: *It's not life if it's lived in fear.* That's the quote.'

I stood, stunned. My partially decomposed hands shook out of embarrassment about both my ancestors and my misquote.

Corina was right. I didn't want to live in fear, but nor did I want to get discovered as some freak, then locked up or thrown into a museum of oddities or burned at the stake. But there was another reason I felt shaky; Ernesto had been right.

I was totally in love with Corina Parker.

And I was unprepared.

Amanda reads all sorts of sappy romance novels about mortals in love with vampires, dark fairies, werewolves and even witches, but my comic books had nothing to offer in terms of romantic advice. NinjaMan just didn't have any experience on crushing on a vegan vampire who both terrified and exhilarated me. I was going to have to make this up as I went along. I decided that the first order of business was make sure nobody suspected I was a zombie, to protect my friends from any modern-day witch trials.

'I'll be careful,' I promised. 'But what should I do?'

'Cook up a cover story,' she said. 'Okay, tell everyone you moved schools and you're back for a visit.'

'Amanda said half the people at the school came to my funeral.'

'These *people*,' she said, twitching her fingers in air quotes, 'can barely remember what they did yesterday. Just go with it.'

'If you say so.'

'I do say so,' she said, opening the door to the bustling corridor.

'Corina?' I asked, stopping her in the doorway. 'Do you really think I'm a moron?'

'The jury's out,' she stated. 'You're new to being unnatural and there's a certain amount of moronicness that's to be expected. Nothing personal.'

I huffed. 'So long as it's not personal.'

'Look, Adam, I've been this way since I was born. And I was probably a moron when I was a little bloodsucking baby, but I grew up and grew out of it. Now it's your turn zom-boy.'

'So I'll see you tonight?' I asked. 'Same place?'

'If you're lucky, I'll float down at three,' she said. 'Ish.'

'Cool, I'll be there.' *It was a date!* 'Hey, do you really sleep in a coffin?'

She looked over her shoulder as a wave of students passed the door. 'Did I say that?'

I nodded. 'You said it wasn't soundproof.'

Corina sighed. 'My mom's parents are orthodox, very traditional. They gave it to me on my Vein Day.'

'Your what?'

'It's kind of a right of passage for my type.'

'Like a Bar Mitzvah?' I asked. I was less than a year away from mine, though I wasn't sure where the Torah stood on a young zombie becoming a man.

'I guess,' she said. 'But with bloodsucking instead of a band.'

'And presents?'

'Usually human body parts, but I asked for money instead,' Corina explained. She straightened her leather jacket to leave. 'I bought this with the proceeds.'

'You look good in Prada,' I said.

She smiled. She actually smiled. It was good to see her smile.

I was a bit jealous that Corina had a family tradition about her vampirism, even if it did lead to her sleeping in a coffin, which, I can attest to based on personal experience, is a claustrophobic way to get one's zzz's.

'Hey, can you bring more Pop Rocks tonight?'

She tapped her pocket and I heard the telltale sound of plastic-wrapped candy. 'Never leave home without 'em, zom-boy.'

7

In Which I Get the Assignment of My Afterlife

My first class was science and my teacher, the Hamberger (Mr Hamish Berger, part German, part Scottish . . . does that make him Germottish?), hadn't changed in three months.

Literally.

I don't think he had actually changed his clothes since my fatal bee sting. He wore the exact same yellow and brown* checked shirt under brown leather overalls. Hamberger had fiery red hair to match his fiery temper, but I cut him some slack because he was the one teacher who had manners enough to address me in the formal way.

'Nice to see you back, Mr Meltzer,' said the Hamberger as I filed in to class. The students gawked

---

* I'm not fashionista, but yellow and brown together makes me think of pee and poo and that's got to be a runway no-no.

at me like I was a ghost. I was tempted to correct them, but kept the truth to myself.

I was surprised to see that my desk was empty, but I suppose no one wanted to sit at a dead kid's desk. So I took my old seat on the far right of the room, opened my new notebook, and waited to write down some learning.

'But you're not on the register any more,' he noted.

'That's okay, Mr Berger,' I interrupted quickly. 'I'm not really back, just visiting from, um, my new school.'

The Hamberger narrowed his eyes and stuck out the tip of his tongue in his 'I'm thinking' position and finally said, 'Mr Meltzer, I don't mean to be insensitive, but you died and I sent flowers.'

He had me there, but I wasn't going home to house arrest without making a stand. 'Well, it's kind of top secret, but I witnessed a mafia hit and went into the Witness Relocation Program. The Feds faked my death.'

'Co-oool,' shouted Allen Doogle from the back row.

'Uh huh,' nodded the Hamberger.

'Yeah, and now the trial's over, I thought I'd sit in on my favourite teacher for a few days while I'm visiting.'

'Very well,' he said. 'I'm glad you're not dead, but you owe me a bouquet of flowers. Or nine-ninety-nine plus interest.'

My impromptu Witness Protection story wasn't an elegant lie, but it seemed to have worked. I spotted Ernesto across the classroom rolling his eyes at me. *Like he would do much better.*

Satisfied, the Hamberger looked out over the entire class and clapped his hands together to get our attention. 'The school board is insisting on something called "student-led learning", where you kids pick your science project. To me, it sounds retarded, but—'

'You can't say that,' said Alexa Miller, our know-it-all class president. 'It's offensive to retards.'

'Actually, Alexa,' I said, raising my hand. 'If he thinks it's actually *retarding* – the verb – our learning, he can say that. But it's not okay to call someone a *retard*.'

My cousin Jimmy, my dad's sister's middle kid, was retarded. That was the term we all used in the family, and Auntie Grace said that was the proper term to use. But calling someone a *retard* was really mean. Jimmy was about five years older than me, but acted about five years younger. He was in a special needs school and I understood that he'd always need help, even into adulthood, but I loved Jimmy and not just because I taught him to be as compulsive with hand hygiene as me. He wore his emotions on his sleeve and told you to your face what he thought of you; which was usually something like 'I love you' or 'you are awesome'. Sure he had the table manners of a seven year old, but I'd never met anyone with more positivity. The world would be a much nicer place with more Jimmys in it.

The Hamberger nodded to me. I think he was happy I was back. 'Anyway,' he continued, 'I want you all to suggest study topics about an ecological phenomenon. Could be climate change, could be water quality, could be—'

'Cow farts,' said Allen Doogle.

'Enough of yer lip,' snapped the Hamberger. 'Other suggestions?'

'Plight of the polar bears,' said Amy Hocking.

'Pesticides,' shouted Tommy Walker.

58

There was only one phenomenon I was interested in: bees. I raised my hand again and said, 'Killer bees.'

'That's just an internet rumour,' Hamberger said dismissively.

I was about to correct him when he paused in thought. 'Bees,' he mused. 'The world's population of bees is dwindlin' and no one knows why. Good topic, Mr Meltzer. Are the queen bees losing command of their hives? Is it Tommy's pesticides? Overwork? Is something messing with their antennae; their sense of direction?'

'Playing Xbox, yo,' Allen shouted from the back.

'Shut your mouth!' the Hamberger billowed. 'And keep it shut if you have nothing worthwhile to contribute.' He certainly hadn't mellowed since my time in the W.R.P.

I knew that ecologically speaking the disappearance of the bees was bad news, but I must admit, and I'm not proud of this (but if you can't be honest in your memoirs, when can you be?), that at that moment, all I was thinking was: *Take that you filthy bees! You kill Adam Meltzer, you deserve to disappear!*

But I wanted to know what happened to me, and

why. Was there a zombie-making killer bee on the loose?

I wrote in my notebook: *Where can you bee?*

The next class was English, and our teacher, Ms Talon, welcomed me back to class by shoving a well-worn paperback of *To Kill A Mockingbird* into my hands. The book's cover was frayed, snot-stained and I'm pretty sure had mostly been read in the toilet. I retracted my hands from receiving the germ-infested novel. The book slammed on to the scuffed linoleum.

'Pick up Harper Lee's masterpiece,' Ms Talon said with a scowl.

'I'd like to buy a new copy,' I said.

'Just pick it up, Adam.' It wasn't a request; it was an order. But one I didn't want to follow.

'Off the floor?' I asked.

She nodded. I resisted. We both stood over the fallen book. It was a standoff.

Ms Talon tried to project a look of laid-back, festival-going hippy-chic with her vintage ankle-length dress and thick brown hair held in place with a chopstick, but I saw right through the façade. She'd been brainwashed at teacher's college to become an authoritarian tyrant thrusting 'worthy reads' into the hands of a generation raised by the Disney Channel.

We both stood there, neither of us making a move. Who would break first? The standoff was only broken when one-eyed Topher Edwards waltzed in, spotted the book splayed spine-up, and scooped it up like it was a ten-dollar bill[*].

Perhaps it was his missing left eye that would have alerted him to the snot stains.

'Very well, Adam,' said Ms Talon. 'Turn up tomorrow with a pristine copy of *Mockingbird* and be ready to read.'

'Thanks, Topher,' I said.

'For what?' he asked, bumping into a desk before taking his seat by the window.

The rumour was that Topher Edwards sucked his left eyeball out with a vacuum cleaner while being babysat by Angie Malcolm, who was too busy making

---

[*] There's a saying that money is the root of all evil. I for one believe that the true meaning was lost in translation. Money is the root of all germs. It's proven that coins and bills are the biggest transmitter of surface-borne germs. NinjaMan Forever, volume 346, featured the evil Greenback poisoning the ink used in the money-printing process to infect everyone.

out with her boyfriend to notice what toddler-Topher was doing. But my mom, who was Topher's doctor, claims that while doctor–patient confidentiality prohibits her from revealing Topher's true ailment, it had nothing to do with a Hoover and, knowing my neuroses, promises it's not contagious. I take Mom at her word, and yet I've noticed that Angie Malcolm has never been asked to babysit in the Meltzer household. Not even once. The truth, much like glassware washed without rinse aid, remains cloudy and unclear.

Unlike in science class, where my desk went uninhabited, my back-row seat in English had been taken over by Bobby 'Buttcrack' Bethal. Robert Bethal had a bad case of what's often called 'plumber's butt'. In the seated position, Bobby displayed his crack to anyone unlucky enough to be behind his behind.

In most classes, Bobby was smart enough to sit in the back row to avoid the teasing and sniggering. On the first day of English class back in September, he'd been stuffed in a locker by some of the football players from the adjoining high school (we shared an auditorium, gym and most disturbingly, locker rooms) and was late for class. He ended up in the second row from the front where 70 per cent of the class had to endure his plumber's butt.

On that first day of class, I had selected the back row for two reasons. First, Ms Talon had chronic bad breath from too much coffee in the staff room. And second, I really didn't like reading books that weren't graphic novels. By my maths (a subject I *did* enjoy), if a picture was worth a thousand words, and one page of a 'proper' novel was two hundred words, and assume the same space could display four comic-book quality picture panels, then each page of literary prose wasted 3,800 words[*]. The inefficiency was staggering, bordering on offensive.

But sometime during my coffin-cation, Buttcrack had pounced on my back-row real estate. But I wasn't going to make a fuss. Bobby needed the spot more than I did. Since it was probable that his bare butt cheeks had rubbed on the wooden seatback at some point in the past three months, and school

---

[*] Maths time! One page only has 200 words on it. But if the same space had four comic-book style panels, and each picture is worth 1,000 words, then that's a potential of 4,000 words. Therefore, each page of prose-only literature wasted 3,800 words of pictorial potential. Q.E.D.

budgets being what they were, I was pretty sure the janitorial staff had never once given the seats at Croxton Middle School a wipedown in fifty-two years. Of course, I had a pack of antibac wipes in my backpack. I disinfected his old seat and sat down. In my spiral notebook, I wrote: English Class – *How to Kill a Mockingbird*.

As Ms Talon recited a depressing passage about a girl called Scout who spent most of her time playing in the dirt and bushes without a care for basic hygiene or for insect-borne diseases, I doodled all the ways to kill a mockingbird:

- Baking them in a pie, nursery-rhyme style.
- In a blender.
- Aural assault from Amanda's playlists.
- Going back in time to snuff out their eggs.
- Mockingbird vs NinjaMan in caged match. No contest.

'Adam Meltzer,' the teacher called, interrupting my creative free-flow. 'Perhaps you'd like to share with us what Atticus Finch means by walking in another's person's shoes?'

Besides the fact that I'd been asked how to kill a mockingbird, not a finch, why on Earth would anyone want to put their feet in another person's shoes? All sorts of hidden dangers lurked in the damp darkness of a stranger's footwear.

'Ms Talon, I don't think Atticus has ever heard of Athlete's foot*,' I said. 'Or nail fungus or even just garden-variety foot sweat. He may be a brilliant lawyer, and some kind of literary beacon of civil rights, which are both noble undertakings, but you should never slip your feet into someone else's shoes. It's just asking for a whole shoe-full of trouble.'

She pursed her lips in disapproval. 'Adam, your sarcasm—'

'What?' I asked. *What sarcasm?* I was being completely serious. If I were being sarcastic, I would've told Ms Talon that I adored her True Blood fan fiction I found online under username @talonclawsbites.

'—is unhelpful and amounts to disruptive non-subordination.'

'You mean *in*subordination?' I clarified.

---

* Not the sole purview of athletes, you should know.

'Out!' she commanded, pointing at the door.

'What did I do?' I asked.

'You know darn well,' she said. 'Now, up, out and down to the principal's office.'

I packed up my mockingbird death list, slung my backpack over my shoulder, and walked out very confused. I wondered if I needed a lawyer to defend myself. Maybe Atticus Finch would be available once he found his shoes.

8

In Which I Go to the Office
(For the First Time)

The meeting with the principal was downgraded to a brief check-in with the vice principal, Mrs Santanton, whom the entire student body called Mrs Claus behind her back because she looked like a female Santa Claus. Mrs Claus was a frequent flyer at the Croxton Doughnuts & Biscuits drive-thru, but her fatty layers hid a heart of gold.

'So you rubbed Ms Talon the wrong way?' she asked.

'I didn't touch her,' I said, holding up my hands.

Mrs Claus laughed. She had a round belly, that shook when she laughed, like a bowl full of jelly* (and doughnuts).

* A nod to probably my favourite poem, 'Twas the Night Before Christmas'. Dad used to read it to us every Christmas Eve. When I was younger, it scared me so much that I couldn't sleep all night; the idea of a bearded stranger mounting a home invasion through the chimney, assisted by a getaway car made of enchanted reindeer – chilling stuff.

'But I think I insulted her,' I admitted.

'That apple bruises a little too easily,' said the veep. 'She just got her fiftieth rejection letter from one of those big New York publishing houses, so she's a bit fragile today.'

'For her fan fiction?' I asked.

'Truly dreadful,' she said. 'I don't advise reading it.'

'I found them online,' I admitted.

'Then you've had punishment enough,' she said, hefting herself up from behind her desk. 'It's good to have you back, Adam. But now that you're out of the Relocation Programme, you don't need the disguise.'

'Hmm?' I wondered.

'The make-up.'

'Oh, is that obvious?'

'A little bit, cover girl.'

I couldn't admit that underneath the powdered foundation and ruby rouge was grey, decaying skin. 'Old habits, I guess.'

'Why don't you spend the rest of the class in the library? Give Ms Talon a wide berth today. I'll show you the door.'

I always found this adult ritual – of showing me

the door – very odd. I mean, I knew exactly where the door was. I just walked through it to get into the room. How else would I be there? Or perhaps she wanted to show me the door like it was some special possession or a trophy, they way I might show off a limited edition NinjaMan figurine or Japanese vinyl bear: hey, look what I've got – a door; betcha haven't seen one of these before? It opens *and* it closes.

'Thanks, Mrs Cla—' I stopped myself from saying 'Claus'. 'Thank you, Mrs Santanton.'

'Don't worry,' she said. 'I know what the kids call me. When you get to my age, Adam, the double-fried donuts just taste too good to stop.'

'I suppose,' I said, walking through the door that I was just shown. 'Thanks all the same. I think you'd make a really good principal.'

During class time, the hallways of Croxton Middle School were lonely and desolate places. As I walked down the locker-lined hall of A-wing to the library, I noticed that the lockers had had a colourful makeover while I was away. Instead of the monotone beige, the dented metal lockers now boasted every colour of the Pop Rocks Island Fiesta pack. It made me think of Corina. Maybe Nesto was right; I did have a thing for her. Until then, my only real crush was on our librarian, Mrs Kundak.

I opened the automatic doors to the library by tapping my elbow to the handicap button and entered a sanctuary of sanity. I loved the library. It smelled of computer fans and disinfectant and while I still didn't like to actually touch the shared books on the shelves, it was the one place on school grounds that my mind felt free to roam.

'I heard you were back,' said Mrs Kundak. 'You had this town in tears.'

'Sorry about that,' I said. It was weird to think that people actually cried over me, Adam Meltzer.

Mrs Kundak strolled around the library counter and opened her arms for a hug. But she quickly remembered that I didn't go in for human-to-human contact.

'I almost forgot,' she laughed.

She raised her right hand for a faux high five. I waved my palm past hers and we pretended to slap hands. It was our thing.

'But you didn't,' I said. 'Thanks.'

Mrs Kundak wasn't that old, maybe mid-twenties, and she pulled off a vintage 60s look that gave

Croxton Middle School a dose of style that most teachers could only read about in fashion magazines. She decorated the library with lava lamps, bulbous paper lanterns, and replica mid-century modern furniture. We both shared a love affair with the IKEA catalogue. Yep, I was into her.

And I think she liked me too because she always put out the industrial strength tube of antibac wipes on the counter whenever I walked in. I didn't know anything about Mr Kundak, and never asked, but my mom once uttered that he was 'bad news'.

'Are you here for pleasure or punishment?' she asked, pushing up her tortoiseshell glasses*.

'That's a big question,' I said, thinking about my return to the land of the living. 'I'm not too sure actually.'

'Well Mrs Claus just rang and said you could probably use a few minutes to regroup before facing Talon's claws.'

'You've read her stuff too?'

She pointed her finger down her mouth, faking a

* Not actually made from any body parts of tortoises, turtles or other sea life.

71

puke. Usually, body humour would send me running, but there was something about Mrs Kundak that made it charming.

'But you know you have to face her eventually,' she said. 'What's she got you reading?'

'*How to Kill A Mockingbird.*'

'*To Kill a Mockingbird,*' she clarified. 'Stick with it, Adam, it'll grow on you.'

'Like fungus?'

'Like mind-opening, soul-expanding fungus.'

I shivered.

She pushed up her glasses again. 'Now, what's really on your mind?'

Just about everything was on my mind, all at once. Life, death, TV shows I'd missed, Corina, the killer bee, Nesto's germy hands, but most of all Corina.

'You're a woman, right?' I asked.

'Last time I checked.'

'So, what would you want someone who's got a crush on you to do about it?'

'If this is about . . . me,' she said hesitantly, 'I legally have to call the guidance counsellor and maybe the police and get lawyers and all that.'

'No, not you,' I said. Was it my imagination, or did

she look disappointed? 'No offence,' I added.

'None taken, Adam,' she smiled. 'Who is the lucky lady . . . or maybe lucky—'

'Corina Parker. I think I might have a thing for her, but she's pretty mean to me.'

Mrs Kundak sat down on a big red cube and motioned to me to do the same. 'Adam, I've met your parents and as much as you might think they can be a pain, they are loving, grounded people who care deeply for you and your sister—'

'This has nothing to do with my sister—'

'What I mean is,' she explained, 'is that not everyone is so fortunate. Corina's pretty gruff on the outside because I suspect she doesn't get the love and support that you do at home, that you probably take for granted.'

'Maybe,' I said, realising that I didn't actually know anything about her home life.

'Take a walk in her shoes, Adam.'

'She wears boots,' I said. 'With big heels. And spikes.'

'You know what I mean,' she said with a smile. She rose to show me the door. 'As much as I'm glad you're back from the relocation programme, relocate yourself back to English class and find out why Harper Lee is a genius.'

'Okay, thanks, Mrs Kundak.'

'You're welcome,' she said, hitting the disabled button to open the doors for me. 'Oh, and Adam. It's "Miss" now.'

As I stepped back into the Fiesta Pack hallway, I realised so much had happened in three months. Mrs Kudak was single. Amanda stole my room. Mom donated my clothes to charity. And Dad threw himself into his cult-like self-help book. NinjaMan faced new nemeses, movies came and went, Croxton Middle School chose its Mini-Prom theme (Children of the Corn), and the new IKEA catalogue came out. I'd missed a big chunk of my life, but I didn't understand why. But I wanted to find out, and I'd start with the bee that killed me.

9

In Which I Recruit My New Best Friends

It was pitch black and the smell of sealed, treated wood was making me light-headed. I was suffocating in the fumes; dying. Really dying. I was in my coffin and I couldn't get out. I thrashed against the hardwood roof of the coffin and kicked against the walls of the death-box.

Beep-beep-beep.

And then I fell on to the floor.

I'd rolled right off Lumpy Cot and hit the shag carpet with a thump. As I stood up, I realised I was alive and in the basement. Two rectangular, turquoise eyes of the dryer pierced the dark, watching over me. The machine blew fabric softener freshness through the room, wafting away the horrible fumes of my nightmare.

I fumbled for my Robo-Rhino alarm clock on the floor and silenced its beeping. It was three in the morning.

I hadn't really stopped to think about what death meant to me. My waking up in the coffin and stumbling home happened so fast, that I didn't fully take stock of the horror of what had actually happened. Sitting there in the dark, pulling on a sweatshirt over my brand-new NinjaMan PJs (thanks, Mom!), my immortal wake-up call came back to me:

I'd never been close to a grave before (before I was in one, I mean). My grandpa died when I was eight while competing in an over-60s hot-dog eating contest. It wasn't even an official competition, it was Spring Training. They called it the 'Grapefruit League' but I'm sure he'd be alive today if they were downing citrus instead of processed pork. Needless to say, Grandpa was a large man and his body was cremated so that my dad and uncle didn't look weak while struggling to carry his coffin*.

Again thanks, Mom and Dad, for not throwing me on the bonfire! I was really lucky to be alive . . . ish. And since I wasn't cinders and ashes, I figured I owed it to myself, and to everyone, to find out what happened to me and why.

* That's not the official story, but I know it's the truth.

76

And I'd need my friends to help me.

I limped up the stairs, my muscles still tight from my dream-time coffin confinement. I opened the screen door to the back yard to find Corina throwing Pop Rocks into the air. Chupa-Nesto leaped into the air to catch them in his slimy lizard jaws. It was like a SeaWorld trick for tweenage monsters.

'Heads up,' said Corina, free-throwing a Pop Rock for me to catch with my mouth. It fizzled so good.

'Good catch, zom-boy,' she praised. I realised that made her the trainer and Nesto and I compliant seals. But who was I to argue when carbonated sugar was involved.

'You okay?' asked Nesto. 'We heard a scream or something.'

I didn't want to get into it. 'Just a bad dream.'

'The one where your mom forces you to make your bed,' Nesto chirped.

'That's a mother who cares about instilling good habits,' I said.

'What was the night-scare, zom-boy?' asked Corina.

'I was trapped in my coffin,' I admitted.

'At least you got out of yours,' she said. 'I'm stuck with mine.'

'You could just sleep on the sofa or something,' I said. 'Maybe ask for a new bed for Christmas. The new IKEA catalogue is out and the JEF line looks sleek and functional.'

'My family would fuh-reak,' Corina said. 'And besides, we don't really *do* Christmas.'

'Technically neither do we,' I said. 'But Mom and Dad didn't want us to feel like outsiders in Croxton.'

'We're kind of all outsiders,' said Nesto. 'Aren't we?'

We were. 'Monsters, freaks . . . outsiders,' I said.

Maybe Ernesto and Corina could understand what it was like to be different from the 'normal' population, but at least they looked normal on the outside.

'I want to find the bee,' I said.

'What bee?' asked Corina.

'The bee that killed me. Then maybe I can understand why this is happening to me.'

'Yeah, you can't become un-undead,' said Nesto.

'No,' I said, realising it was too late for me. 'But we might be able to stop it happening to anyone else.'

But there was more to it. I did want to find that bee, but I also wanted to understand if there was something *wrong* with me. I didn't just die, I came back. I was really confused. I mean, why me? Of all the people who have lived and died, why was I suddenly back from the dead?

It was different for Ernesto and Corina; they'd inherited their conditions and had a good long while to come to grips with their *specialness*. Me, I had specialness thrust upon me by a bumblebee stinger. I wanted answers and I suppose deep down underneath all my decomposing flesh I wanted to know if I could ever be *me* again.

'Maybe there's a way to undo it?' I mused. 'To be normal again.'

Corina scoffed. 'Who needs normal?'

'Yeah,' agreed Nesto. 'You don't hear us complain.'

But my friends weren't being completely honest with me or with themselves.

'Nesto, you complain all the time about not being a wolf,' I said. 'And, Corina, you're hiding from the world out of fear of being experimented on. C'mon, guys, you wouldn't change your, well, um, your *situation* if you could?'

'It would be cooler to be a wolf,' admitted Nesto.

'Way cooler,' agreed Corina. 'And yeah, I'd change my parents if I could.'

'You see? Look, I don't know what we're going to find, maybe nothing, but if the bees had something to do with my death and zombie life then I at least want to try.'

'You're right, Adam,' said Corina.

'I am?' I said with surprise.

'We'll help you,' she said.

Nesto nodded. 'Yeah, us monster-freak-outsiders gotta stick together.'

And it might just get me an A in science.

10

In Which I Take Lunch

The lunchroom at Croxton Middle School on Tuesday was, as usual, like a bustling watering hole in the desert. Animals of all shapes, sizes and cleanliness huddled together to ingest food and affirm the pecking order of middle school life.

I looked around at the swarming mass of humanity, gorging on their feedbags, and noticed something was different. The MocaCoke machines were gone.

The middle school and the high school, the conjoined twins of local education, used to have a deal with Moca-Cola to have MocaCoke machines in the lunchroom and sold at Friday night football games. In return, Moca-Cola built us a new stadium to watch the Croxton Crocodiles battle for pigskin supremacy with the likes of the Fairfield Foxes, Dayton Dragons and Golden Heights Gilgabeasts. But now, the sugar-pushing machines were gone, replaced with a table stacked with milk and water and staffed by an eighty-year-old escapee from the nearby retirement home.

'Where's the MocaCoke?' I asked the lady, whose name tag identified her as Madge. At first I wondered if maybe she was undead like me, but when I reached to take my milk carton I smelled the telltale whiff of cigarette smoke and realised she'd simply made one too many unhealthy choices in life.

'Where you been, kid?'

'Relocated,' I said.

'Bunch of parents petitioned the school board to get sugar drinks banned from school property. So now it's milk or water. What'll it be?'

I refused to drink anything from anyone's udder. 'Bottle of water, please.'

Water in one hand and hermetically sealed* Supperware box in the other, I scoped for somewhere to sit.

Amanda and her lookalikes were gossiping at the

---

* It means airtight, so no germs or bacteria can get in. It's pretty much the best thing since sliced bread . . . unless of course sliced bread came packaged in hermetically sealed bags. That would be better.

table nearest the stage. For a moment, I thought about joining her just to annoy her, but decided that my revenge for her room-stealing should be more imaginative than that. I'd bide my time.

I spotted Ernesto over by the windows with a gaggle of sixth-grade pals. They mostly spoke in one-syllable sentences ('Yeah?' 'Yeah.' 'Cool.' 'Yo.' 'Man.' 'Sweet.') and maybe it was my death-induced vacation, or maybe it was the magic of Harper Lee's words, but I wanted more sophisticated conversation than sixth graders could provide. I settled for a wave, and his return wave let me know he was okay.

I'd hoped to see Corina, but she was nowhere in sight. I made a mental note to ask her where she eats lunch, but remembered that she probably doesn't. Pop Rocks are a portable 'food' and didn't require a tedious forty-five minutes in the lunchroom. She was probably on the roof dining al fresco.

'Meltzer man!' called a voice.

I looked over and spotted Jake O'Reilly pumping his hand in the air. He was proudly holding an illegally imported bottle of MocaCoke and trying to get my attention. Jake was what teachers called 'big boned' but what kids rightfully called 'fat'. He was also going through an unfortunate tussle with puberty, which, judging by the pimples populating his chubby face, he was currently losing. But Jake was a good guy, and since I didn't know where to sit, a sight for dead eyes.

'I'm so glad you're not dead,' he said, standing awkwardly as if he wanted to hug me. With my hands full, I didn't give him the opening. 'I heard 'bout the WRP, Meltz, you gotta tell us all about it.'

Jake O'Reilly was the only person who called me Meltz, which was one more person on the Earth than ideal. But I joined him at his table with Allen Doogle, Philip Frazer who we all called 'Phaser', and Olivia Wolaski was a girl trapped in a gamer's body.

'Yeah, how were the digs?' asked Phaser. 'They put you in a big house?'

I'd created a lie and now I had to feed it. But I figured the best food was the kernels of truth. 'Pretty small, actually,' I said, thinking back to the claustrophobia of the coffin. 'I think they call it *bijou*.'

'Did you get a new name?' asked Olivia.

'I really can't say,' I lied.

'Xbox or PlayStation?' asked Allen.

I shook my head. 'Neither.'

'Effin' Feds cheaped-out on a Wii? Man, why do my parents bother payin' taxes?'

Jake shook his head. 'They want you to risk your life to testify against the mob and then don't even spring for decent digs or console. *Typical*.'

Jake's biggest observation on the world was that things were typical. Typical of what, I never knew. But to Jake, being typical was a major offence.

Two eighth graders walked by and we instinctively cowered to avoid having food thrown at us. One of them, a tall guy I think called 'Cade' nodded and said, 'Nice one taking on the mafia, Messler.'

'You can upgrade to our table, if you want,' said his friend.

'Maybe tomorrow,' I said. 'I've got my sandwich all set up here.'

Jake's jaw dropped. 'They're popular and they just talked to you, invited you to sit with them.'

'You should go,' said Olivia. 'I would.'

'Disloyal,' snapped Allen. 'Minus two points.'

'Just being honest,' she said.

'Um, Meltz,' mumbled Jake. 'Did the Feds dress you up as a girl?'

'Oh, the make-up,' I realised.

'You'd make a cute girl,' said Olivia.

'I can't really go into details about what does or does not happen in Relocation,' I said. 'I'm just happy to be home.'

'But you're like three months behind on Ninjas,' Jake said. 'But don't worry, I've been goin' every week and you can catch up on my stack.'

I nodded noncommittally. I didn't like reading someone else's used comics. I'd turn to the internet for a catch-up.

'And tomorrow's Wednesday, yo!' Jake shouted, shaking his MocaCoke.

He and I had a mid-week ritual of hitting Croxton Comics and Hardware Store for the latest NinjaMan release.

Jake twisted open the blue cap and suddenly the soda erupted, spraying all over my hair, face and T-shirt. I was soaked with sugary syrup. Jake laughed his head off, like he'd been carrying Old Faithful around in his pocket. I didn't find it so funny.

'Oh, so sorry, Meltz,' he said. 'My bad.'

Ya think?

But before I could lie and tell him that it was

all right, Mr Paulson, the gym teacher assigned to lunchroom duty, intervened.

'O'Reilly! Meltzer!' he called, rushing over and discovering the smuggled soda. 'What's with the banned substance?'

'It's refreshing and stimulating,' Jake said.

I made the mistake of licking my lips and a jolt of sugar and caffeine shot through my system. I shuddered, sodden with adrenaline-igniting cola.

'Meltzer, first of all, welcome back. I'm glad you didn't shy away from your civic duty. Someone's got to put these mafia menaces in their place, and while I'm glad it's not me, I sleep a little safer at night knowing that our government is willing to sacrifice others in pursuit of justice. Well done!'

'Um, thanks, Mr Paulson,' I said.

'Second, O'Reilly, I don't ever want to see you with one of those drinks again. Now, Melzter, hit the showers,' he ordered. 'You're dripping.'

Normally, I didn't need to be told to take a shower. If I could, I'd shower five times a day, just to scrub off the grime that hung in the air. For example, did you know that when someone farts, particles from their butt actually float around in the air? So when you smell a fart, those particles are actually nestled in your nose? The official population of Croxton (not counting undocumented aliens and tourists) is 21,371, and that's a lot of butts doing a lot of farting, creating a lot of particles that cling to your hair and skin. If you ask me, five showers a day doesn't seem like enough when surrounded by over twenty thousand fart-producing butts, but the one exception I made was for showering at school, especially during lunchtime.

'But sir,' I said, using the word 'sir' to appeal to his authoritarian nature, 'isn't it the high school's football practice hour? I can shower at home later.'

'Yeah, it's not like it's dirt,' said Jake.

'You're covered in cola,' said the teacher. 'And it'll attract bees and rats and—'

'What kind of bees?' I asked, wondering if there was some link between my killer bee and banning of syrupy soda from school grounds.

'The buzzing kind,' he said. 'Listen, we finally licked that rat infestation in the staff room so we'd really like to keep a clean bill of health with the board.'

Amen to that. But I still didn't want to brave the locker room at lunchtime.

'Grab a T-shirt from the spares bin,' he said, 'and hit the showers.'

'You mean the T-shirts that other people wear?'

'Don't be a Nancy, Meltzer,' he said. 'Hit the showers or stay here and clean up the lunchroom with O'Reilly. That's his punishment.'

'Mr Paulson!' Jake protested as the teacher snatched the half-empty bottle from his hand.

'O'Reilly, get the mop. Meltzer, hit the showers. I ain't asking.'

Jake and I looked at each other, resigned to our fates.

11

In Which I Face the Football Team

I never liked the locker room during what Mike +
the Mechanics* called my 'living years', but now the
prospect of entering the public school equivalent of
the torture chamber filled me with dread. It was bad
enough that I had to rummage in the spare T-shirt
bin for a used grey 'Property of Croxton Athletics'
shirt. Now I had to face the locker room we shared
with the high school kids at a time when no sane
middle schooler would dare enter.

I paused at the door. Since I was three months
out of circulation, I had no way of knowing if my
personal protection racket was still intact . . .

You see, at the end of last semester, I was still

---

* A (non-make-up-wearing) rock band my parents liked. To the best of
my Wiki-knowledge, not one of them had ever fixed a car.

grade-A bully fodder. One day the football team were practising plays in the locker room with me as their pigskin when Brock Turner, the star quarterback, came in and warned the locker room: 'Nobody touches Meltzer until I graduate!'

The football team had gently dropped me to the floor, where I counted three pubic hairs that were not attached to anyone's pubis, and I took comfort in the knowledge that I had at least another semester left of the protection racket.

'You okay, Meltzer?' Brock had asked.

'That's a broad question,' I'd said. 'But yes, I'll live.' Of course, I was being overly optimistic; but just didn't know it.

'Brock on!' he'd said, a phrase that he was literally trying to copyright. I had helped him with his application at the trademark and copyright office*.

In fact, I'd been helping Brock Turner with a lot of things: Algebra, chemistry, his college football scholarships, and even how to tie a tie (the team

---

* The decision is still pending. But if approved, you'll owe five cents to Brock Turner. Email me and I'll send you the payment details.

suits up on game days, and fine motor skills are not Brock's forte).

He and I would make a good team if my life were a buddy cop movie. But as much as I'd like to think that we were friends, he was in high school and I was in middle school. We were allies of convenience, that's it. I helped him with intellectual matters and he provided a kind of no-fly zone over the Meltzer melon.

His mom worked at the local pharmacy and my mom sent all of her patients to her to fill their prescriptions. I overheard Mom on the phone to the pharmacy owner once threatening to take all of the practice's business somewhere else if Mrs Turner ever got fired. There was a type of elegant symmetry in the relationship. My mom was providing a protection racket for Mrs Turner; Brock was watching out over my physical well-being, and I was protecting his intellectual pursuits.

As I stepped into the locker room for the first time in my zombie form, I stepped over the pubic hairs and headed straight for my favourite peg. Only it wasn't there.

In its place was a laminated yearbook photo of me with the words 'Adam Meltzer Memoreal Peg' lovingly misspelled above my sixth-grade yearbook picture.

It was a touching tribute, but not entirely helpful. Now I had nowhere to hang my soda-soaked shirt.

'Yo, Meltzer,' called my imaginary big brother.

'Hey, Brock,' I said, turning to see him return from practice.

'What happened to you, little dude?' he asked. 'You look like sh—'

'Shower time!' called another voice.

'Last one in feels the wrath of the towel snap!' yelled another.

The buffalo herd had arrived.

'Whoa,' called Smash, the giant linebacker. 'I heard you was still alive.'

'I is,' I replied, attempting to speak bull.

'We all got the morning off school for your funeral, so thanks for dying-like,' he said.

'Any time,' I said with a wave as the bulls followed the red cape of hot showers. Brock stayed behind.

'Seriously, Meltzer,' he said. 'You really freaked me out. I cried, you know.'

And then Brock punched me. He actually reached out his right arm at high velocity and whammed me in the shoulder. I think he meant it as a physical display of brotherly affection, but it dislocated my shoulder.

'G-ahhhh!' I cried. 'What did you do that for?'

'Jeez, Meltzer,' he said worriedly. 'Did I hurt you?'

I winced through the pain until I realised that if I could feel pain then I could feel. My nervous system was still operational. I was dead, but I could still feel. I didn't understand the biology of the undead, but the fact that I could still feel, even if it was abject pain, made me smile.

'Why you grinnin'?' asked Brock.

'I'm grinning,' I said. 'Because it's good to be back. And, Brock, you don't get a discount for dropping the 'g', so when you're in your college interview, go full freight. Grin-ning. Not: grinnin'.'

'Thanks, Meltzer, I'm glad you've got my back.'

'I do, Brock. Even if you almost cracked mine.'

'Ah, walk it off,' he said. I stared. 'That's what the coach says to us.'

So that's what I decided to do. Just walk it off. In fact, I decided to make that my mantra for my entire zombie afterlife.

Walk. It. Off.

'I'll try that,' I said to Brock.

But I still wanted answers to how I became the walking undead.

12

In Which I Upset Dad
(For a Good Cause)

That night at the dinner table, it didn't take long for the conversation to move from what we learned at school to poo.

'Have you had a bowel movement yet, Adam?' asked Mom as she passed the potatoes.

'Grossmeout!' gagged Amanda.

Dad tapped Mom's knee. 'Darling, maybe we should keep the doctor talk to the clinic?'

Ya think?

'I just want to get to the bottom of Adam's digestive tract,' explained Dr Mom.

'MOM!' shouted Amanda, covering her ears. 'I can't listen to this.'

Mom ignored my sister and turned to me. 'Well, have you?'

'No,' I admitted. 'But I haven't really had a moment's peace, have I? And the IKEA catalogue's missing from under the sink and you know how—'

'We're *EATING!*' gagged Amanda. 'It's bad enough I have to look at you!'

'I thought you weren't listening,' I said.

'Well, you just keep me in the loop,' Mom said, giving me a wink like we were in a secret poo pact.

'OhMyGod, can we please talk about something else?' Amanda pleaded, uncupping her ears. 'Dad, say something interesting, or cos it's you, probably boring. Whatever!'

'They're cutting my research funding,' he announced.

'Oh, not again, dear,' Mom sighed.

'Julius just doesn't prioritise the Arts. He's built another science facility and apparently research into medieval literature just doesn't excite the alumni.'

Dr Julius Austin was once my dad's friend and even golfing buddy, but now he's the president of Croxton University and Dad's boss. And Dad is still, in his own words, '*babysitting* undergrads"*. I figured

---

*   Undergrads: that's a fancy university word for students. Professors, I've learned from my dad, don't like to see or talk to them. Which I can understand: apparently they don't shower very much.

that's why he's so obsessive about his management guru books. He really didn't want to be in his former friend's shadow any longer.

'I'm sorry, sweetheart,' said my mom. 'I appreciate your research, and you kids do too, right?'

'Get with the programme, Dad,' said Amanda. 'Medieval lit died out with CDs.'

Jeez she could be insensitive.

'Sorry, Dad,' I said. 'Lots of people still use CDs. But they're mostly old people.'

'He's already got six science buildings,' Dad lamented. 'And he just built these enormous greenhouses on the north side of campus for some experiment with growing giant flowers. Something to do with the bees apparently.'

'Bees?' I said, perking up, not only eager to ensure the conversation didn't return to poo, but *maybe Dr Austin could help*. 'I'm doing a science project on bees. Do you think you could ask him to let me see the experiment?'

As the words left my mouth, I realised too late that I was twisting a very painful knife in Dad's back.

I hoped for answers to how a bee put me in my premature, albeit temporary, grave. What if the killer bee was still out there, poised to strike again. I didn't know what to think, but I did know I had to find out more.

Little did I know that this one impertinent* request would bring about the end of the world.

That night, I found Corina and Nesto perfecting their Pop Rock toss-n-catch in the back yard, but was too geared up to join in.

'I think I've got us a lead on the bee,' I said. 'My dad's ex-best-friend-turned-arch-academic-nemesis is doing some kind of big experiment on bees at the university, and we should check it out.'

'Really?' asked Corina, catching a Pop Rock. 'And how are you going to get into a university science laboratory, genius?'

'Not me – *we*. And since I'm back from the dead, I'm pretty sure I've got a week to ask my parents for anything I want.'

---

* Impertinent: it's an adjective, a describing word, and kind of means rude, or out of place. In this context, yeah, I admit it – I was out of line to ask about connecting with Dr Austin. I heard this in a movie once and it stuck with me. Feel free to use it!

'A car!' shouted Nesto.

'Go on,' said Corina.

'I know it's manipulative to play on my dad's guilt over burying me and all that, but—'

'They're parents,' scoffed Corina. 'They're meant to be manipulated. They respect it. Like puppies and school bus drivers.'

'Well . . . anyway,' I continued, 'I think I can get my dad to get us into see Dr Austin. He's pretty much the smartest guy in town. If he can't help me, no one can.'

13

In Which I Get Physical in Maths

By Wednesday, I was starting to get used to being back at school. Sure, I still got strange looks and plenty of questions about being protected by the Feds, but the school's news cycle had moved on from Adam Meltzer's mysterious reappearance to other matters like the graffiti on the staffroom wall and the sighting of Moca-Cola vending trucks circling the school grounds. Adam's return from Relocation was old news.

But at least my street cred was up a notch. I didn't feel any different, but I could tell people were noticing me more. I got more 'hellos' and 'how's it goin's' in the hallway than before my death. Maybe it was the zombie thing; maybe it was that since seventh grade was drawing to a close I was almost to the top of the middle school heap. It hadn't even been a full week yet, but I liked being back at school.

After three months of brain hibernation, it was nice to give my noggin a workout. I could almost feel my grey matter getting beefier. And the fact that I could remember things from one day to the next meant that my brain wasn't as decomposed as Amanda insisted it was.

I aced a pop quiz in science class and the Hamberger said he was glad the mafia didn't rub me out. I really appreciated that kind of teacher support.

English class even improved. I made up, in a matter of sorts, with Ms Talon, by reading ahead in *Mockingbird*. I was hoping the book was going to be a kind of Mary Poppins tale whereby Atticus would bring in a prim and proper (and ideally flying) British nanny to tag-team with Calpurnia to whip Scout and Jem into shape . . . and insist on regular baths. I kept that plot-twist fantasy to myself and simply shared with Ms Talon that Harper Lee was making me a better person. It was a peace offering, and she accepted it.

But things didn't add up so nicely in maths. What should have been a simple lesson about exponents erupted into a fracas about the difference between projected human population and potential human population. This was the one class I shared with Corina and when I said 'Hi' to her on the way in, she'd made it clear we were to maintain our pre-death distance at school.

'Let's not arouse suspicion,' she'd said.

So even though I sat across the aisle from her, she ignored me. I looked over at Jake in my old seat with buyer's remorse.

My teacher, Mr De Datta, our 'guy from Mumbai' was explaining the mathematical concept of exponential growth and used human population as an example. It was all well and good (except of course if you're worried about how steep the hockey stick[*] is) until I suggested that we also ought to calculate the potential population. Mr De Datta corrected me, explaining that the 'projected population', including births and deaths, was already included in the population formula.

I put up my hand again to explain that it was the

[*] I don't do contact sports, but the hockey-stick effect in graphs means that something starts out by only growing a little bit and then all of a sudden takes off and grows really fast. Amanda's snarky attitude is a case study in this.

deaths we should treat as 'potential'. After all, bodies in graves are just zombies waiting to wake up.

My comment raised a big chuckle from the class, a death stare from Corina, and a stern look from Mr Shrivatsa De Datta.

'I may be from Mumbai,' he said, 'but that does not fly.'

Mr De Datta really liked to rhyme things with Mumbai.

I wasn't going to admit to being among the risen dead, but since maths was supposed to be based on factual truths and not subjective opinion, I thought that we should use all of the most current, up-to-date info we had on hand. And since I was a zombie who was less than a week old, my very existence was current and up-to-date.

'You're trying to be a funny guy,' he said.

'No,' I said. 'I wouldn't even try.'

The class giggled.

Guy.

Try.

I honestly didn't mean to make a Mumbai rhyme.

Jake leaned over and whispered. 'Are you gunnin' for class clown?'

'Did you sniff your hand sanitizer this morning, Meltz?' called the incumbent class clown, Terry Finklestein, from the back.

He always sat in the back.

Terry's real name was Terrence but everyone called him Finkly. And he'd carved out the class comedian role for himself. His jokes were funny, his heckles were hilarious, and he had an uncanny way of working with the teachers, not against them. He was comedy genius in the way that he made the class laugh and never got suspended.

But he was possessive of his top spot on the stand-up (well, sit-down) Croxton Middle School comedy circuit. He did not take well to challengers. And he clearly saw me as a challenger. I'd clearly upset the balance of the seventh-grade universe by being funny on his turf.

I turned to find Finkly smirking a kind of 'I-dare-you-to-take-me-on' smirk. His thick black hair was bleached blond and his thick black glasses made him look like an angry movie critic or one of those guys on TV who'll buy your gold with no questions asked. I shrugged.

'You don't sniff it, Terrence,' I explained. 'You

just apply it thoroughly to your palms, thumbs and between the fingers. You can have one of my bottles, I buy in bulk, because I know sometimes you forget to wash your hands after using the bathroom.'

Finkly dropped his smirk and fired back, 'You want an early grave?'

'Been there,' I sighed, turning around to face our guy from Mumbai.

But suddenly, I felt a tug at my hair and Finkly dragged me into the aisle between desks, and started punching me.

It didn't hurt so much as felt uncomfortable, like dental work under local anaesthetic*. Terrence Finklestein landed four punches as the class chanted, 'Fight, fight.'

I decided to practise non-violent resistance since I was pretty sure he'd just hurt his still-living hand on my dead skull. I looked up to see Corina rolling her eyes in disapproval.

'Oh my!' called Mr De Datta. He stormed between the desks and grabbed Terry, who started to bawl.

'Principal's office,' he ordered. I looked up from

---

* The needle that really stings but then makes your mouth all numb.

106

the floor and held up my unclenched palms in utter confusion. 'You know why.'

Mr De Datta walked both of us down the hallway to the fishbowl office and deposited us on the hard sofa.

'These boys need to be seen by Mr Eriksen following an altercation in my classroom,' he said, returning to preach the logic of mathematics to thirty students who were just cheering for blood.

The school secretary, Miss Cooper, who could barely see over her desk, looked up at me and said, 'We don't have frequent flying points, you know.'

'You come here lots?' asked Finkly, shaking his head in disbelief and wiping a stray tear from his cheek.

'It's been a hard week,' I said.

'Tell me about it,' he said.

'Wish I could.'

'Yeah,' he said with a sigh.

'So, why'd you unload on me?' I asked.

'I'll tell you,' he said, 'if you tell me why it didn't hurt. You didn't even flinch.'

'Maybe you're a better comic than a boxer,' I said, slipping a smile.

'I landed four good 'uns on ya,' he boasted. 'You're not even bruised.'

'It's a new diet,' I lied. 'I'm eating better.'

'There's something weird going on with you. Did they do, like, experiments on your in the relocation programme?'

'Nah, but it does toughen you up a bit.'

'I could use a bit of that.'

'Everything okay at home, Terry?'

He turned away.

We'd had a lesson in health class about violence in the home and one of the telltale signs of domestic violence was bullying at school. So I worried that maybe the Finklesteins were roughing him up at home.

'Because if anyone's ever bothering you,' I said, 'you could come over. You're only a block away and my mom always laughs at your jokes. You'd be playing to a friendly crowd.'

'I'm not getting beaten up, Meltzy, if that's what you think,' he said, shaking his head, inhaling a sniffle. 'So just leave it.'

'Then what is it?'

'It's my mom,' he said.

I have to admit that I was surprised. I never liked

his dad's desert-dry sense of humour, but never thought his mom would lay a finger on him.

'She's dying,' he added.

Now I felt let like an idiot. The Finklesteins were supposed to be friends of my parents, but aside from dog walks and friendly waves as our cars passed on the road, we hadn't seen them since I was in fifth grade.

'And you said that stuff about people in graves, and—'

'I'm really sorry, Terrence,' I said. 'It was a stupid thing to say. I wasn't thinking.'

'No, it was cool and funny and I dunno, a part of me wished I'd thought of it. Maybe that's what made me more mad.'

'It was a doofus thing to do,' I said. 'And I'm sorry.'

'You didn't know,' he said. 'She's got cancer and probably hasn't very long left. And when she goes, it'll just be my dad, my brother, and me, and there's no coming back from the grave. No "potential population".'

I felt stupid, doofus-stupid. Of course I didn't know what he'd been going through. My zombie quip was just a bit of silly showing off.

The principal's door opened and Mr Erik Eriksen, a hulking man who was rumoured to partake in violent Viking re-enactments, stood menacingly in the doorway, beckoning us in like judge, jury and executioner.

We both stood, resigned to our fates.

But Miss Cooper interjected. 'Mr E, I think these two just had a simple misunderstanding and there's no need for any punishment or record of their incident. I think it's best they return to class.'

The principal looked slightly shocked by how direct and assertive the mousy school secretary was, but nonetheless took her direction as edict.

He looked relieved to retreat back to his paperwork. 'Yes, yes, looks as though you two boys have patched things up, so run along back to our guy from Mumbai.'

As I turned to leave, I caught the secretary slip me a slight nod and a subtle wink. Miss Cooper clearly had some leverage over the principal and had just used it to help us.

I put my arm around Terry's shoulder as we stepped back into the hall and he crumbled. It turned into a full man-hug.

Terrence Finklestein may not wash his hands after doing a number two, but right then I knew he, and I, needed to focus on the big stuff.

Big stuff, like finding that killer bee before anyone else had to die.

14

In Which I Return to Mecca

The problem with Wednesday afternoon is that you have to wait all day for it. But the school bell finally rang and I met up with Jake for my first post-death comic-book run. Jake caught me up on three months of NinjaMan adventures. He'd been nearly killed eight times, captured twice, and shot to the moon once. NinjaMan, that is, not Jake. Jake O'Reilly hadn't left Croxton in ninety days and the biggest thing that had happened to him (aside from his best friend dying) was that he finally finished the two-thousand-piece puzzle of the pyramids. He was very proud.

The ding-zing-wong NinjaMan-themed door chime welcomed us into the holy temple of Croxton Comics and Hardware. I was a bit worried that it just wouldn't feel the same in my afterlife, but as soon as we walked in, it was as if nothing had changed.

The store was run by twin brothers, Robert and Lee, who were like opposite sides of the same superhero identity. Lee, who was clean-cut and fussy, ran the hardware side, while Robert, who possessed a Zen surfer approach to life and dress, ran the comics side.

As I entered the shop, I felt ready to get back on the comics horse. Of course, I'd never willingly go anywhere near a horse – covered in fleas, constantly attracting flies, and able to kill you with one swift kick of a hind hoof. But you get the idea.

'Adam Meltzer has risen from the grave!' called Robert in his south of the Ohio River drawl.

How did he know?

I felt like I was kicked by a hind hoof.

Would he call the authorities?

Corina's paranoia filled my brain. I didn't want anything bad to happen to her or Nesto, and I certainly didn't want a Guantanamo holiday any time soon.

'Um, no I didn't, that's impossible,' I stuttered, spitting out the lie. 'No one can rise from the grave. I mean zombies aren't real, so how could anyone—'

'R-aaargh!' grunted Jake, raising his arms and deadening his eyes in a mock-zombie attack that I considered to be just a little bit racist.

'Ree-lax, Adam,' Robert said. 'Jakey told me all about the WRP. I guess you're a little on edge, aren'tcha?'

'Scarface wanted him D-E-D, dead!' said Jake, dropping his zombie impression. Why was it okay to make fun of zombies?

A part of me wanted to just come right out with it: *I'm a zombie!* But I didn't. I kept the undead part of me hidden under layers of MAC foundation.

'Must be nice to be out in the world,' Robert said.

He had no idea. Or did he?

'Better than being stuck in a safe house,' Jake said. 'Or was it a bunkhouse?'

'More like a split-level ranch,' I said, imagining the Brady Bunch home from TV reruns. 'But I don't really want to talk about it.'

'That's right, guys,' mused Robert. 'The past is the past, and there's no point revisiting it.'

Jake raised his hand like he was still in school. 'Unless you have a time machine!'

'Even then,' said Robert, 'the past will mess with you if you mess with it. The future, that's where the future's at. And your future starts now.'

He pulled two copies of NinjaMan volume #1,685

from the shelf and placed them reverentially on the glass counter. 'I've been to the future,' he said, tapping the comics, 'and it's awesome.'

'I can't wait to read it!' Jake said. He plunked three crumpled singles on to the counter. They were so filthy that they looked like he used them for face cloths. 'I'm going to pretend my mom's meatloaf gives me food poisoning to skip soccer practice to read it tonight.'

'Jake, your mom doesn't brown her meat. It's a recipe for food poisoning.'

'Cheryl shoots for speed,' said Jake. 'Cooking gets in the way of her programmes. Want to come over for dinner?'

I shook my head. I've never met anyone less interested in food hygiene than Jake's mom. I take a packed supper with me every time Mom ships me off to their house. Their kitchen is like a shrine to salmonella. The O'Reilly family runs large, and Jake's no exception. They've got big bones, thick skin and I guess sturdy constitutions. Me, I'm wiry and sensitive.

'Cheryl's probably outside,' Jake said. 'You sure you don't want to come for dinner?'

'I'm positive,' I said. I didn't just want to avoid the ER, I also wanted to follow up Dad about that meeting with Dr Austin.

'Okay, later, Meltzer!' he called, disappearing through the ding-zing-wong door chime.

I carefully opened my softened Italian leather wallet and pulled out three crisp dollar bills. I laid them on the counter in fan formation and took #1,685 and placed it into a plastic file folder I pack in my backpack every Wednesday morning.

'Thanks, Robert,' I said, turning to leave. My own family's dinner was in my future.

'You're secret's safe with me, Adam,' he whispered.

I stopped but didn't turn around. *I think he knew what I really was.*

'I know what you are,' Robert said, 'and it's cool.'

'I gotta go,' I gulped. 'It's spaghetti night.'

He totally knew.

15

In Which I Go from Middle School to College

School blew by on Thursday because I was so focused on getting to the university. Despite the bad blood, Dad got me an appointment with Dr Austin and so after school, Corina, Nesto and I walked across town to meet Dad's mortal enemy . . . and hopefully the man with answers to my buzzing questions.

Officially, we were on a school assignment to understand the plight of the bees, but unofficially, there was just one bee I was interested in; the bee that killed me.

It was time to solve my own murder.

'Thanks for coming with me, guys,' I said.

'Homework's way more fun when you don't do it at home,' said Nesto.

'No problem, zom-boy,' quipped Corina. 'Beats staying in with my parents, watching the decapitation channel.'

As we crossed Main Street and followed the mislabelled Elm Street* to the edge of campus, it felt good to have my new friends with me on my quest. Naturally, I was the most prepared of the group. I had packed my backpack with my notepad, an emergency preparedness kit (matches, water purification tablets, Band-Aids and iodine), a large tube of moisturiser (Nivea gets my vote for creaminess, ease of application and overall pleasant scent), extra foundation (once you've gone MAC, there's no going back) and of course, plenty of hand sanitizer.

Nesto's bag was filled with food, if you call processed meat twisted into balloon animal shapes 'food', and a pair of toy binoculars he won in a piñata.

'What are you carrying?' Nesto asked Corina.

'This isn't even my assignment,' she said. 'My job is to look good and let lesser people do the carrying for me.'

'Lesser people?' I clarified.

'I meant shorter people,' she said.

'She's got us there, Adam,' said Nesto.

Corina had stuffed the pockets of her Prada with

---

* Entirely lined with oak trees.

Pop Rocks, so she wasn't totally useless. And, if I'm honest, she did look great. And smell great too. I caught a whiff of Corina's perfume and inhaled. She smelled of grapefruit and toilet cleaner; it was pretty irresistible.

'Did you just sniff me?' she asked.

'I like your perfume,' I said.

'It's sunblock,' she said. 'SPF 150.'

'Wow,' I said. 'And I thought I was well protected at 60. That's the strongest they carry in the pharmacy.'

'I've got delicate skin,' she said, 'so I get it from Vamazon*.'

I leaned in slightly and took another sniff.

'Don't ever do that again,' she warned.

'No one ever sniffs me,' Nesto said as we crossed on to campus. 'Well, 'cept for dogs, but they only sniff my butt.'

'So what exactly are we looking for?' Corina asked.

We walked up the main boulevard of campus. I pointed to a large building at the end that looked like a castle. With its turrets, drawbridge and

---

* Like Amazon, but just for vampires. Apparently they've got the best prices on coffins on the web.

119

waterless moat, the university administration was the strangest building on campus. Dr Austin's office was on the top floor, in a turret.

A bald mannequin of a woman called Miss Bellweather showed us into the president's office where we sat waiting on an oversized leather sofa, surrounded by a dozen bronze busts of great scientific minds perched on pedestals. I recognised Albert Einstein, Charles Darwin, Watson & Crick, Marie Curie, Isaac Newton, Thomas Edison, Benjamin Franklin, and that guy who invented the home rotisserie-chicken machine.

'Future scientists!' Dr Austin boomed as he marched into the round room, rubbing the top of Einstein's shiny bronze curls. 'That's what we need here,' he continued, flashing a news-anchor smile with teeth so bright I wished I'd brought sunglasses. He wore a white lab coat open over his three-button suit, presumably for scientific street cred.

'We are men and women of science, ready to rein in Mother Nature, to bend her to our superior human will!'

I could see why Dad didn't like him. He was loud, brash and confident; everything my dad wanted to be but wasn't.

But I was a fan and he had me from '*future scientists*'.

'Meltzer the younger, I expect you know that your father and I do not see eye to eye on the priorities of a research institution, but that matter is between us grown men. I have every intention to nurture your scientific curiosity and save you from the dead-end path of liberal arts. Same goes for you –' he looked down at a piece of paper with the famous snake-biting-the-apple Croxton U logo on it – 'young Master Ortega, and Mizz Parker. Say, say, you're not the daughter of Tony Parker, DDS*, are you?'

'Dee-dee yes I am,' Corina said with a smirk.

Austin flashed his blinding smile again. 'He keeps my pearly whites, well, pearly.'

Ernesto, squinted his eyes. 'And really white.'

'Looks like you could do with a date with the dental chair, young man.'

Ernesto clamped his mouth shut. He looked down awkwardly at the beige carpet. I had a hunch that his full-moon gorging didn't contribute to a healthy mouth environment.

---

* DDS stands for Doctor of Dental Surgery. Personally, I think dentists should call themselves 'dentalists'.

'I'll report back on the status of your teeth,' Corina said. 'Pearly and white.'

'Wonderful,' said Dr Austin. 'Now that we've dispensed with the socially acceptable though time-consuming pleasantries, I will inspire your young minds to scientific greatness.'

He proudly plucked a copy of his autobiography, *Worldshaper*, from the shelf and started to sign it. We used to have a copy until Dad accidentally dropped it in the fireplace.

'Um,' I said, firmly taking charge of the meeting. 'We're doing a project about bees.'

Suddenly, he slammed the book shut and swallowed his smile. Nobody said anything.

I shifted on the leather sofa, piercing the awkward silence with a distinctive fart sound.

'Really?' cursed Corina.

'No, no,' I said, 'It wasn't a—'

Nesto interrupted me with laugh and I caught a scowl from Darwin*.

---

* He's the guy that says we're actually descended from apes. He's not very popular at Nesto's church because they believe in something called 'intelligent design', which I limit to IKEA. I mean, there's nothing intelligent about impending puberty. But Swedish flat pack, that's intelligent and stylish.

Dr Austin straightened his lab coat. 'I'm sorry children, but I cannot help you.'

'But,' I protested. 'My dad says you're doing experiments with flowers and bees and that—'

'There's been a gross misunderstanding here—'

'Exactly,' I said. 'That sound was the leather rubbing against—'

'Miss Bellweather will show you the door.' He reached under his desk and must have pressed the *get-the-annoying-trio-out-of-my-office* button because the freakishly statuesque Miss Bellweather reappeared to show us the door.

'I've seen one before,' I said as she swept us out of the room.

She shut us out, ending our quest before it even *bee*gan. But there was something going on and I refused to give up.

I descended the circular stairway of Dr Austin's ostentatious castle, defeated but undeterred. But my friends were less enthusiastic to continue.

'Oh well,' sighed Ernesto. 'Let's just use Wikipedia like normal people.'

'We're not normal people,' I said. '*Remember?*'

'I am so going to get Dad to give him a root canal

next visit,' Corina said viciously. I made a mental note of her vengeful streak.

'They are doing bee experiments,' I said. 'My dad wouldn't lie – he doesn't know how.'

On the walls of the staircase, we passed framed photos of Dr Austin with famous people and world leaders. I felt bad for my dad. His nemesis was the super-successful university president with his own castle and my dad was still stuck in the classroom. But what was Dr Austin really up to?

'He doesn't want us, or maybe anyone, to know about his experiments,' I said. 'He's hiding something.'

'Not his teeth,' said Corina.

I was starting to get a bit dizzy, looking down, going round and round, when we finally reached the ground floor.

'Did you see his face when I said the word "bees"? It was like I'd shaken his hand without washing it first.'

'That's only a thing with you,' said Ernesto. 'How come you're such a clean-freak anyway?' He hit a little too close to the decomposing bone.

'So my teeth don't have rodent flesh stuck in them,' I snapped back.

Nesto clamped his mouth shut again and hung his head. He sulked off to examine his teeth in the reflection of a portrait of Dr Austin hanging in the main lobby.

'Say sorry,' hissed Corina.

'Sorry, Nesto,' I said, pulling some dental floss from my pocket. 'Here, this stuff's industrial strength.'

'Thanks, Adam,' he said, holding the floss like it was radioactive. 'I'm sorry too. I know you just like to keep things neat-n-tidy.'

'Okay, very nice, boys,' said Corina. 'Adam's right. Pearly Whites has something to hide and I smell a rat.'

'Oooh, really, where?' asked Nesto. He looked around excitedly, licking his lips.

'Let's not get distracted,' I said. 'We need to investigate.'

I walked out of the castle, over the waterless drawbridge to a map of the university. The map was partially papered over with a flyer for tomorrow's SMOOCH concert. I ripped it off the map and pointed to the north-east corner of campus. Beyond the stadium that would stage Field of Screams tomorrow was a greyed-out zone marked 'future development'.

'Right there,' I said. 'That's where Dad says the new research centre is. That's where we should look.' I unfurled the flyer in my hand. 'Tomorrow, when everyone on campus is distracted by the social event of the season.'

16

In Which I Find My Rhythm Again

Last year, when I auditioned for the school play, I only landed a part in the chorus because they didn't have enough boys. The experience was the beginning and ending of any Broadway aspirations I'd harboured (and honestly: who hasn't?).

For my audition for the school musical, *Bye Bye Birdie*, I'd prepared a monologue from *Our Town* and completely blown it. I was nervous, sweaty and forgetful. Mr Mojuan, the drama teacher we shared with the high school, pulled me aside afterwards and said, 'If you can sing, kid, you've got a chance, but your acting was more wooden than the boards.'

Mr Mojaun, whom we all called Mojo, seemed to feel that Croxton Middle School musical theatre was just a few steps off Broadway. He claimed to be from New York; but we all think he meant the state and not the city.

I wasn't allowed to even finish my vocal auditions. Mr Ealson, the music teacher, stopped me mid-song to repair the broken window*. It was humiliating, and not to mention dangerous with all those shards of glass everywhere.

But in my dance number, I didn't just cut some rug – I'd shredded it. In the theatre world, I'd be known as a *single* threat.

So Mojo reluctantly gave me a part in the chorus under strict instructions to lip synch. Technically my character's name was Town Teenager Number Three, but as far as Mr Ealson was concerned, my role was to 'shut up and dance'. I got to swing and sock-hop onstage and discovered an artistic outlet that dovetailed with my desire for order, control and symmetry. Dancing required discipline, precision and a total commitment to routine. I was made for it.

At the start of seventh grade, when the school musical got announced – this year it was *Anything Goes* – Mojo wasn't so generous. 'We need triple threats, Adam,' he'd said.

Anything, it seemed, did not go.

---

* I still maintain that a bird smashed into the music-room window.

'But this is the only school club that doesn't involve full body contact,' I'd pleaded.

'What about the chess club?' he'd countered.

'You kidding? I went to one meeting and Francis Miller tried to gouge out Temperance Taylor's eye with a rook. No, no, chess club isn't safe.'

'Have you considered activities outside of school, Adam?'

Mojo introduced me to the Croxton Sunshine School of Dance and I took my single theatrical talent off campus. For once a week, for ninety minutes, I gave myself over to the Thursday night ritual of choreography.

There were eleven of us in the class, and I was one of only two guys. The other one lived on a farm and came to Sunshine under an assumed name: Nathan Detroit. In class, Nate, who was two years older and at least a foot taller, was one cool customer, but I knew (and he knew that I knew) that he'd get his head handed to him in whatever Hicksville High School he attended if word got out that his Mom drove him into Croxton for dance class. I'd once seen Nate in town coming out of Icy Al's Used Sports Emporium, with his dad, hauling hockey equipment. Neither of us said 'Hi'. Outside of Sunshine, we were total strangers. But inside, we were stars.

When I got home from campus on Thursday, Mom surprised me with the news that she'd contacted Sunshine and they'd welcome me back. I reminded her that since she'd paid the fees in advance, technically I'd be welcoming them back.

'Adam, do you want to go or not?'

After the week that I'd had, I relished returning to the normality of black spandex and show tunes. My dead feet were itching to boogie.

The class was rehearsing a new routine that I would have to catch up on, but our teacher, Phatima (she'd legally replaced the F), cheered my return with a the Sunshine School chant:

Step up for sunshine;
Step hard for thunder;
Step loose for the spotlight;
Step out for wonder!

We dived straight into the new (to me) choreography – the opening number from *Cabaret* – and I forgot all about zombies, vampires and chupacabras. Between pivots and leg kicks, I started to feel normal again.

After rehearsal, high on endorphins* and show tunes, I decided that I wanted to talk to Corina – to see where I stood with her.

I suffered through dinner with Amanda complaining about some bizarre love triangle emerging in the eighth grade involving her BFOTW (Best Friend of the Week) Cammy, herself and a guy named Trigg who should be in high school by now but was held back for a middle school victory lap.

'What do you see in this Twigg?' asked my mom. 'He sounds like an underachiever.'

Being an underachiever was a cardinal sin in Mom's books.

'It's Trigg, and he's the best. But if he takes Cammy to the concert then she'll, like, automatically be his date for the Prom.'

'Let him drive Camero to the concert,' I said. 'If you go with Mom and Dad, they'll support your liquorice habit.'

'Adam, did you dislodge your brain at dance camp?' she said. 'You don't know anything about anything.'

---

* It's your body's way of making your feel good. Kinda like sterilizing a counter top. Nothing better.

131

'You two are siblings,' said my dad, stating the obvious. 'You love each other. Act like it.'

'Amanda, dear,' said Mom, 'if you love someone, set them free.'

Maybe that's why Corina was always so mean to me; maybe she felt about me the way I did about her.

'Are we talking about Adam or Trigg?' Amanda asked. 'Because I've been leaving the front door unlocked for years hoping that Adam would run off and find another family to feed him.'

'I'm not a stray cat,' I said.

I took a last mouthful of Dad's meat loaf and decided to walk out of the unlocked door to see if Corina really was just trying to set me free.

17

In Which I Have a Date with Corina

When I rang Corina's doorbell, I expected something spooky, like tortured screams. But all that answered back was a soothing *ding-dong-ding* door chime. Her dad, Dr Parker DDS, opened the door with his one arm and said, 'Say ah.'

'Ah,' I repeated.

'Open wide so I can see what the problem is,' he said, trusting his hand into my mouth and peering at my no-longer-so-pearly whites. He was dressed in all white. White pants, white belt and a white button-down collar shirt with the left sleeve sewed shut just below the shoulder.

'Um, Doccer Parrer, I'm naw here for a chess up,' I said without closing my mouth.

'What can I do for you?' he demanded. 'Magazine subscription? Donation to a local cause?'

'I could pre-book an appointment for my

liquorice-dependent sister, but actually I'd like to talk to Corina.'

'Why would you want to talk to *her*?'

That wasn't quite the response I was expecting. 'She's my friend,' I said.

'She's sulky, snarky and ungrateful,' he said.

As he insulted my new friend, I glanced past him to peer into their house for the first time. Their living room had every piece of seating furniture covered in protective plastic. Their bookcases and shelves overflowed with knick-knacks. A row of Franklin Mint plates decorated the walls above the doorframes. I'd put the Parkers down for minimalist chic, but their house was downright tacky.

Mrs Parker swept into the hallway, wearing a long black gown. She looked ready for a funeral or auditions for goth mother of the year.

'Gets it from her mother,' Dr Parker added under his breath.

Corina's mom swooped though the hallway, but upon seeing me, pretended to be embarrassed. 'Oh, young man, you've caught me in my pyjamas.'

'I wear NinjaMan,' I said.

'I'm sure you do,' she said with a plastic grin. Her

face was bleach white with two strokes of rouge on her cheeks. I was curious what brand of make-up she used (so I could avoid it), but Corina's parents were creeping me out too much.

'Is Corina home?'

'Where else would she be?' asked her mother.

Of course, I thought it was a rhetorical* question.

But she didn't. 'Young man,' said Mrs Parker. 'Where else do you think she could possibly be?'

As far as I knew, Corina snuck out each night and flew wherever she wanted. With the power of flight, she could pretty much go anywhere. But as much as I was upset and confused by her, I didn't want to get her in trouble.

'Maybe the library,' I said. 'They're open late on Thursdays and it's a great place to do homework if you don't care about bacteria that lurks on shared table tops.'

'Our daughter at the library,' laughed Mrs Parker. 'That is amusing. *You* amuse me, Adam Meltzer.'

---

* Rhetorical question: It's a question that doesn't expect an answer. Like, 'who's the greatest superhero ever?' It's so obvious, that it doesn't require a response.

'Thanks,' I said, though I really didn't mean it. 'Please tell Corina that I stopped by.'

I turned to go, but stopped myself. I really didn't like how mean her parents were to Corina behind her back. It was petty and unfair. I had no doubt she could hold her own if she was present, but in absentia*, her character was being assassinated.

I spun back around before the dentist and the goth could close the door and stood up for my friend.

'I think you guys have got Corina all wrong. She's really smart, super savvy, and yeah she's a bit sharp edged, but it's a sharp-edged world. And I for one am a big fan.'

I spotted Corina emerge on the first-floor landing behind her slightly shocked parents. She was wearing an identical gown to her mom's, presumably her pyjama gown, and leaped over the banister and floated down to the tiled floor of the front hallway.

She burst past her surprised mom and dad. 'Later.' Corina glided on to the front porch. I couldn't tell

---

* In absentia: It means not there. Kind of like Amanda whenever the dinner-time conversation turns to anything worthwhile or interesting.

if she was walking or hovering, but she grabbed my hand and pulled me down to the pavement.

For one exhilarating and terrifying moment, I thought Corina was about to kiss me.

Did you know that the mouth is home to over two thousand forms of active bacteria? It's actually the dirtiest place on the human body (no, seriously, and I am including the back gate in this) and yet it's how unaware lovers greet each other. I mean, if you really cared for someone, the last thing you'd do is greet them by pressing your saliva-soaked lips on to theirs.

'Please don't kiss me,' I said.

'As if,' Corina replied, pulling me down the pavement towards the park. 'I was actually considering hitting you, but figured you'd had enough bullying today.'

'Oh yeah,' I said. 'Thanks for sticking up for me. You've got superpowers and you just sat back and watched as Finklestein took out his unprocessed grief on my face.'

'That was me not drawing attention to myself,' she said.

'I'd pick a different stylist then.'

She looked down at her gown with annoyance

and embarrassment. 'Mother insists that I respect the traditions,' she sighed. 'But my deal with her is that if I wear the gown at coffin time, worship Count and study the scrolls, then I get my own fridge just for my vegan food.'

'Good trade, I suppose.'

'Yeah, I don't want my tofu getting mixed up with their human bone marrow.'

'Of course not,' I said.

'And she doesn't hassle me to attend Sacrifice,' Corina added.

'Sacrifice?'

'It's better that you don't know the details, but friends and neighbours are on the exempt list so your family is safe.'

That was good to know, I thought. We turned off the pavement and into the small wooded area nestled behind a square of houses.

'Ooh, this park is off limits after seven,' I said. 'Except for maybe drug dealers and teenagers.'

'You have *got* to lighten up, zom-boy.'

Before I could defend myself, Corina wrapped both arms around me. *Oh great*, I thought, *she is going to kiss me.*

But she didn't. She lifted us up into the air and perched us along the branch of a pine tree. We were higher than the houses and could see clear across town. The spires and stadium of the university dominated the dusk horizon and for a moment, we just sat in elevated silence.

'This is pretty much my favourite place,' she said.

'You come up here a lot?'

'Most nights,' she said. 'That's the one good thing about sleeping in a coffin. My folks, the drama queen and the dentist, can't tell if I'm in there or not.'

'What if you asphyxiate* in the night?'

'Mother once threatened to install a baby monitor, one of those video ones, but I argued that it violated my civil liberties and I'd take it all the way to the Supreme Court if I had to.'

'You'd probably win too,' I said.

'Dan Wright I'd win,' she snapped. 'Anyway, Mother backed down. She's all show in the house, but she does not want unwanted attention.'

---

* It's a verb, an action word. It means to die from not getting enough air. I didn't know how well vampire-sleeping coffins were ventilated, so it was a fair concern.

'I see where you get it from,' I said, immediately regretting the words as they left my mouth.

Corina punched me hard.

I lost my balance and fell off the branch. I was hoping that one of two things would happen: either Corina would dive off the branch and catch me, or the soft undergrowth would cushion my fall.

Instead, I slammed down hard on an unsuspecting drug dealer.

18

In Which I Crush a Drug Dealer with Maximum Velocity

We'd been taught to 'just say no' to drugs since the third grade, so there was a certain elegant justice to Crash's final word.

'Noooooo,' he cried, as I slammed the guy into the ground.

I crawled off the crushed victim and stumbled back to my feet and took a good look. I recognised him, even in his mangled state.

His name was Carter Saunders, but everyone knew him as 'Crash'. Crash had been kicked out of Croxton High two years ago and had spent his time knocking around downtown and lurking at the school perimeter, offering drugs from his satchel. He always left me alone because my mom had once been his doctor. But he was bad news and the kind of guy that everyone in town wished would just take a one-way bus ticket to Somewhere Else.

And I had just crushed him to death.

Corina floated down to the leaf-strewn ground, now covered in blood. 'What did you do?'

'What did *you* do?' I snapped back. '*You* pushed me.'

'You said I was like my mother,' she said.

'Hardly,' I said, still smarting from Corina's corporal punishment for making even an accidental mother-daughter comparison. 'And you think *I'm* sensitive?'

But Corina was transfixed by the dead body. Crash's corpse was oozing blood from the mouth and I caught Corina lick her lips. She was mesmerised by the sight of the blood. 'What. To. Do?'

'What do you mean?' I asked. 'We've got to call 9-1-1.'

I really hoped I could explain it in a way that would avoid a manslaughter charge.

'He's dead,' she said. 'Look at him.'

And I did. His body was twisted and his mouth gaped open in a dead stare. Ordinarily, I'd be very uncomfortable with a dead body, but now since I was one, I was trying to apply a little love to my kind.

'And you killed him.'

'You pushed me,' I said.

'Is that how you want the police report to read?' she asked. 'Two freaks were sitting in the treetops and one pushed the other to smash the town drug dealer to death.'

I didn't.

'We can't just leave him here,' I said. I've watched enough cop shows with mom and dad to know that if CSI arrived, they'd track me down with one swipe of a fluorescent lamp. I was so on my way to prison.

'No, you're right. Too many questions. An investigation. They'd eventually find us and then . . .'

'They'd take us away,' I said. I didn't think I'd survive Git'mo or Shawshank.

'You're catching on, zom-boy.'

Corina kneeled down beside Crash and straightened out his broken neck.

'I've been off the plasma for three years,' she said, licking her lips. 'And this is not how I imagined my relapse. But here goes.'

She took a big breath and bit into Crash's neck. His soft tissue squished and she slurped his blood. Corina let out a deep moan. I couldn't tell if it was out of disgust, or satisfaction, or both.

Crash's arms flailed and his legs kicked, stirring up the leaves. Corina motioned with her eyes to stop him. I winced at the sight and pinned down the convulsing corpse as best I could.

'Ooooooh,' he screamed, finishing his last word.

Finally, Corina pulled away, blood dripping from her mouth. She wiped the blood from her face with the sleeve of her gown. My first concern was blood-borne diseases. But a close second was stain removal.

'I could've asked Dr Mom to test him for stuff first, you know,' I offered, a few moments too late.

'I'm immune to human diseases,' she boasted.

Flight and immunity. Wow, she really did have the best superpowers.

Suddenly, Crash bolted upright. He was pale, but looked very much alive.

'What . . . what . . . happened?' stuttered the reinvigorated corpse. He held his head and clutched his neck as the bloody wound was closed up, healing itself.

'Hiya, Crash,' I started. 'Well, it's kind of a funny story.'

'I'm not laughing,' he replied.

144

'I saved your worthless life so that your death didn't become a distraction,' Corina said.

'I was . . . *dead*?'

'Sorry,' I said.

'Don't apologise,' said Corina. 'He should say sorry to you for being in the park after hours.'

Crash looked confused. 'Wait, am I dead now? Is this heaven?'

'You're still in Croxton,' I said. 'She turned you into a vampire.'

'Let me explain,' said Corina. 'You are my kind now and I own you. As your maker, I can undo you. So here's what's going to happen if you want to exist on this planet: you'll dump the drug dealing and go back to school.'

'I'm banned from high school,' he admitted. 'Wait, *vampire*?'

'Night school, you moron,' she said. I was suddenly a little jealous that I wasn't the only moron in Corina's life. 'Believe me, you'll like the night a whole lot better than the day.'

'There's some great night-school courses,' I added.

'Vampire?'

'You're a first-stage vampire,' Corina explained.

'You'll be this way for a year and if you clean up your act, I can make you a full member of our clan. Disappoint me and I'll finish what mad Meltzer here started. It's your eternity, Crash. It's your choice.'

Crash stood up, tested his limbs and stretched his neck from side to side.

'What do I do now?'

'Get used to being a vegan,' she said.

He looked awkwardly at me. 'Ooh, isn't that a woman thing?'

'Google it, pancake,' she said. 'Now I'll be watching you. You'll hunger for blood, human blood. If you draw a drop from the human population it'll be a very fast end to your immortality. Now get out of here. Go see my father at his "dentist's office" tomorrow. He'll explain our ways and assign you a blood brother.'

The fact that Corina used air quotes when she said 'dentist's office' did not escape my attention.

'Meltzer, are you a vampire too?' he asked.

'No, I—'

'He's something else,' Corina said.

Crash looked at me, trying to understand what was going on.

'Sorry for crushing you, Crash. It was an accident. Just one of those things. Right, Corina?'

'Just one of those things,' she agreed. Corina pointed to the path leading out to the pavement. 'Out.'

Crash began to amble out and then stopped. 'What were you guys doing up there anyway? Making out?'

We looked at each other. 'Gross,' we replied in unison.

It was nice to be on the same page about something.

19

In Which I Show Off and Find Some Really Big Flowers

On Friday, while most of the town was getting pumped for the big SMOOCH concert, we set out on Mission Beepossible. In the area that was greyed out on the campus map we discovered a mammoth greenhouse structure protected by a tall wire fence.

'This is it,' I announced. But as far as I could see, there was no gate to get in.

I sized up the fence. It was at least twelve metres tall, and I didn't even like standing on a stepladder. But over was the only way in. I was going to have to climb. I pulled a spray sanitizer out of my backpack and spritzed the wire. I couldn't be sure if the last person who'd tried to scale this fence had washed his hands.

Bzzzzz.

The wire sizzled like Dad's illicit bacon. He has a

secret stash in the freezer that he fries up when Mom goes to Sunday morning Pilates.

I looked up and spotted the telltale yellow triangle sign: a genderless, black figure being zapped to death. *Death.* I didn't know if I could die twice, but I didn't want to look like a wimp in front of Corina.

'Good thing I'm already dead,' I said, reaching out and clasping the fence.

Bzzzzzzzzz.

A surge of electricity shot through my decomposing body.

'Ahh-ooh,' I cried as I clambered up the fence one rung at a time, gently frying my insides.

'Hmmm,' sniffed Ernesto. 'Is someone barbecuing?'

I lowered myself back down the other side, I found the electrical box nestled at the bottom of the concrete base of the greenhouse and switched off the juice. I was feeling pretty darn proud of myself.

But any pride evaporated when Corina rose into the air and floated effortlessly over the fence.

'You could have reminded me before I fried myself,' I said.

'What? And rob you of your moment of heroics? You looked like NinjaMan up there, Adam Meltzer.'

'Really?'

'No,' she said. 'You have zero coordination and you looked positively petrified.' My non-beating heart sank. I had tried to be macho and failed miserably. 'But I'll give you a B for bravery.'

It wouldn't win any scholarships, but I could live with a B.

Nesto scrambled up and over the fence. When he jumped down, he landed on all fours like an animal and I wondered if he was about to trans-mutate. But he simply stood up and said, 'I'm hungry. Too bad we didn't find that rat.'

'Probably a blessing in disguise,' I said.

'You should try veganism,' Corina said.

'Ooh, are they tasty?' asked Nesto.

As my friends argued about the merits of animal versus plant matter, I sized up the immense greenhouse. No wonder it was so big; inside were rows and rows of giant flowers.

'You see any bees, zom-boy?' asked Corina.

'Notta one,' I said, 'but we should follow the pollen.'

None of the windows were open but I found a steel door along the outer wall of the glass building that was surprisingly ajar*. By cutting the power, it must've released its magnetic seal.

We walked into a forest of flowers: towering tulips, soaring sunflowers and lofty lotuses. These mega flowers were at least nine metres tall.

'Wow,' panted Ernesto. 'My chupacabra could really go wild in here.'

'Keep Mr Hyde inside,' said Corina. 'We can't let anyone find us out.'

'I can't go chupa on demand anyway,' he said. 'Even though it would love to trash these flowers.'

'My mom would be relieved.'

Suddenly, we heard a buzz and the steel door shut itself. A bank of lights in the rafters lit up. The power was back on.

'And what else do giant flowers attract?' I asked.

'Giant bees,' said Corina.

'Then let's bee-a-huntin',' I declared.

---

* For clarity, it was a door, not a jar.

20

In Which I Uncover Evil

I felt like Alice in Wonderland, walking through the towers of flowers. Well, to be clear, I felt like a non-Victorian, non-blue-dress-wearing, dark-haired, zombiefied male version of Alice. But aside from those small differences, I truly expected to bump into a giant, chain-smoking caterpillar perched atop a sofa-sized fungus.

I didn't.

Adam in Flowerland did, however, hear a *buzz*.

I held out my hands to stop Nesto and Corina from walking on.

'Don't touch the Prada,' Corina scoffed, brushing my hand away from her designer jacket and carrying on.

But Ernesto stopped in his tracks, pointed at my hand, and said, 'Your finger bone's sticking out, you know.'

He was right. A white bone had popped out, leaving the open flesh of my right hand's middle finger just dangling off the bone. It was fleshy and floppy; utterly revolting. I shuddered, but tried to keep calm. I didn't want to touch it, but neither did I want to let my decay get in the way of our Mission Bee-possible.

'Don't be a wuss,' Corina called. 'Just pop it back in.'

'Seriously,' asked Ernesto. 'Is no one else hungry?'

I held my breath and pretended the hollow flesh of my finger was nothing more than penne pasta. I slipped my finger flesh over the bone and made a mental note to ask Mom to sew it up properly. My immediate concern, however, was infection, so it was lucky that I'd packed the emergency kit.*

'Aaargh,' I cried as I doused the wound with iodine (yes, it still hurts a zombie) and wrapped it with two NinjaMan brand bandages.

Buzzzz.

There it was again.

'Did you hear that?' I asked.

---

* Of course, it wasn't luck. It was preparedness.

'You crying like a wuss?' asked Corina.

'I can,' said Nesto, tilting his head, listening intently. 'The buzzing and the wussing.'

'Buzzing,' I declared. 'The buzzing of bees. Underground.'

Nesto bent down towards the ground, right down, until he nearly buried his head in the dirt. 'But bees don't live underground, ants do.'

'So we're looking for bees with an identity crisis,' mocked Corina.

But there was no denying the buzzing was coming from beneath our feet. Ernesto dug though the dirt but only found worms. I caught him popping one in his mouth when he thought I wasn't looking.

'I said I was hungry,' he shrugged. 'But there's nothing down here except dirt and delicious worms.'

'What if there's a secret subterranean level?' I asked.

'You read too many comic books, zom-boy,' said Corina.

But I pushed on through the oversized leaves, discovering a bright red sign on a steel door marked 'SECRET – Subterranean Level'. Maybe it wasn't such a secret after all.

We opened the door and crept down the steel

steps into a large dark chamber. We froze when we heard a familiar voice.

'Meltzer's kid and his two friends were asking about bees.'

It was Dr Austin. I looked at Corina and Nesto for silent confirmation. They both nodded.

'Would you say they were *meddling kids*?' asked a nasal voice, which sounded like a mean-spirited French chef my parents enjoyed watching on TV.

'I would say they were more *inquiring*,' he said. 'And annoying. Meltzer's kid actually farted on my couch.'

I opened my mouth to protest but Corina clapped her hand over it.

'*Meddling kids*,' repeated Professor Plante.

'Michael Meltzer doesn't know anything *sensitive*, does he, Plante?'

'Non! He knows nothing! My work is secret, and you will be pleased to know, nearly complete.'

'All bees accounted for?'

'*Naturellement*,' replied the professor. I couldn't speak French, but I had a hunch he was lying.

'Then we release the hive tonight,' ordered Austin. 'My sponsor wants human trials and they're tired of waiting.'

With that, I heard Dr Austin's footsteps disappear down what sounded like a long tunnel. We crept silently down the rest of the steps to take a closer look. A tall, almost skeletal albino man was hunched over a bank of computers, singing 'Crabs in a Bucket', SMOOCH's number-one hit single, to himself.

His desk was messy, covered in half-consumed cups of coffee, crumpled papers, little pots, jars and tubes, and a handheld video-game system. He had a cluttered pinboard with a big poster advertising tonight's SMOOCH concert. What was it with my parents' generation that they enjoyed people screaming in make-up?

I felt Ernesto's tap on my arm, and he pointed his dirty fingers towards a large panel of glass at the opposite side of the chamber. That was when I saw the source of the buzzing. A swarm of bumblebees, bees as big as walnuts, circled inside a waterless aquarium tank.

There were thousands of them. The big bees looked agitated and angry trapped in their glass hive.

'They're humungous!' exclaimed Nesto, a little too loudly.

The skeletal Frenchman turned around. His eyes

narrowed and his lips puckered like he'd just downed an entire pack of Sour Grape Skedaddles.

'*Meddling kids*,' he squawked, rubbing his hands together.

Wow, I thought. *This guy really loves his Scooby Doo*.

Plante picked up a remote control and the steel door slammed shut. We were as trapped as the bees, stuck in the secret underground lab with a mad scientist with a penchant for Quebecois folk songs and a grudge against meddling kids. I needed a cover story, fast:

Kids on a field trip.

Lost tourists.

Nah, I could do better than that. This guy clearly loved SMOOCH so I'd play to that.

SMOOCH *street team*.

'No, no, no, Professor . . .' I began.

'Professor Plante,' he said nastily. 'The architect of your demise.'

'You've got it all wrong. We're not *meddling*, we're helping. We're a street team from SMOOCH and we just came by to make sure you didn't forget about tonight's concert.'

'What do you take me for?' asked Plante. The game was up. I should have gone with 'kids on a field trip' or 'tourists'.

'That's the best you could do, zom-boy?' complained Corina under her breath.

'Of course I will not forget,' he continued. 'I've been waiting for this concert all year.' *Phew*. He was taking the bait. '*Je me souviens!*'

'And you know,' I said, weaving a new lie, 'the sound check is about to start and all the university professors are invited to hear it.'

'*Sacré bleu!*' he sneezed.

'Godblessyou,' I offered.

'*Merci*, but I have so much work to do here and I cannot leave my lab unguarded. But I've always wanted . . .'

'We'll watch the lab for you, sir,' Corina offered with a fake but convincing smile.

'That's what us street teams are for,' added Ernesto enthusiastically.

Plante's sunken eyes lit up. '*C'est vrai?*'

'It's all part of the SMOOCH service,' I explained.

He quickly turned around and painted his albino face with two parallel red stripes rising from his eye sockets. He checked himself out with a handheld mirror and once satisfied with his SMOOCH look, tapped a few keys on his computer. The screens went dark. He hit the remote control again and the steel door released. The mad professor air kissed us all, shouting '*merci, merci, merci*' as he leaped up the steel steps and disappeared out of the door.

Once we were alone, Corina and Nesto just stared at me.

'What?' I asked, checking myself over. 'Do I have another bone sticking out?'

Nesto laughed and Corina shook her head.

'I can't believe he fell for that,' said Ernesto.

'How'd you come up with it?' asked Corina.

'I saw the poster,' I explained, 'noticed the ticket pinned to his board, recognised the tubes as face make-up and figured he was a big fan.'

'You're smarter than you look, zom-boy,' said Corina. I chose to take that as a compliment.

But I didn't have time to bask. Plante could be back any minute and I wanted to learn what he was doing with those giant bees. I strode over to his computer but the blinking screen demanded a password. My fingers hovered nervously over his filthy keyboard.

'Just try *something*,' said Corina.

'I'll think, you type,' I suggested, taking a big step back from the computer. Professor Plante struck me as hand-washing optional kind of guy.

'Try *password*,' I said. And she did.

No luck.

'Try 1-2-3-4,' offered Ernesto.

Strike two. We had one more attempt left.

'Okay,' I said. 'Try SMOOCH.'

Ding-ding.

We were in. The computer flashed to life with an embarrassing wallpaper of the professor in full SMOOCH make-up and we quickly checked through his most recent files and browsing history. Once I'd sifted through YouTube videos of dancing kittens, maple syrup recipes, and a Facebook page for SMOOCH make-up techniques, I hit evil scientist jackpot.

The folder was called *Death_Defying_Bees*, and a quick scan of its files revealed that Plante was working on the problem of the planet's disappearing bees by making them so resistant to pesticides that upon death, the bees would reanimate and continue to pollenate.

Death-Defying Bees.

He was creating zombies.

Zombees.

But Dr Austin had other plans for the zombees. He'd said something about 'human trials'. I wondered if I was actually the first human trial?

But I didn't have time to do any more digging. The steel door creaked open and Plante was back. He stormed down the steps, looking frazzled and upset. We were really in for it now.

I froze as he marched straight for us and reached out his hand to throttle my throat. But he just reached past me, plucked the SMOOCH ticket from the pinboard and ran off with a renewed spring in his skeletal step.

'He doesn't have a very good nose for meddling, does he?' asked Nesto with his *outside* voice.

Professor Plante stopped. He turned around, finally realising what was going on, and hissed, 'You *are* meddling kids!'

Yes we were.

'And under rule forty-two, paragraph three, subsection double-i of the Unethical Scientists' Union Handbook,' he said, 'I shall have to kill you.'

21

In Which I Make a Daring Escape (Thanks to Corina)

Plante skipped towards us with an evil glint in his eyes and a jaunty spring in his step. He noticed the files open on his computer. We'd seen too much.

Ernesto was distracted from his impending death by the souped-up GameBoy on the desk. 'Wonder what games he's got?' he asked.

'Grab it,' said Corina, suddenly pulling us both close in a surprising display of affection.

I guess we each react differently to the prospect of our own demise. Nesto wanted to spend his final moments trying out a new video game. Corina finally found her emotional on-switch.

As for me, I was preoccupied by whether or not I liked being held by Corina or not. It was nice to know she actually cared, but I wondered if her hug (which was more like a wrestling hold) would upset the delicate nature of our relationship where I was in awe of her and she mocked me. I didn't want our last moments together to be awkward. But she wasn't giving us hugs – she was giving us a lift.

Into the air.

Corina flew us up over Plante's head.

Now, it's no secret that I have always wanted to fly, but the experience of being scooped up by a vegan vampire and cradled over the head of a murderous mad scientist wasn't the soaring first flight I'd always imagined. I should have been the one scooping her to safety.

Nesto, however, literally on the other hand, didn't seem to mind.

'Whee!' he called. 'See ya, wouldn't wanna bee ya!'

We soared over the steel steps and she tossed us through the open door. I tumbled awkwardly into the flower forest.

'Ouch,' I complained, though it didn't hurt anything but my pride.

'You could say *thank you*,' she said. Truth was, I was too embarrassed to thank her. I wanted to fly for myself, not be carried off at the first sign of trouble.

'Thanks, Corina,' said Nesto. 'That was wicked cool!'

'*You*,' she said, closing the steel door, 'are welcome.'

I rose to my feet and dusted myself off with a giant leaf. My ego was bruised and I'm pretty sure my knees were too. But I didn't have time to dwell. Suddenly, I heard a metallic clank. The greenhouse air filled with an ominous buzz.

'Um, guys,' said Ernesto, leaning his ear to the ground again. 'The buzzing isn't coming from underneath any more.'

And then I saw them, hundreds of the walnut-sized bees, swarming straight for us. They looked angry, and determined. I had no idea if these bees were as deadly as my murderer, and even less of a clue what a toxic stinger might do to a chupacabra or a vampire, I didn't think we should stick around to find out.

'Run!' I called.

We raced through the towering stems, dodging overgrown leaves and knife-sized thorns. But the bees swarmed in close pursuit, gaining on us as we fled.

I spotted a row of super-tulips and grabbed at a leaf, yanking it off to create a shield. I handed it to Ernesto and he cowered under the makeshift defence as three mega-bees slammed into the leaf and bounced off.

I pulled down another leaf shield and handed it to Corina. She rolled her eyes and ripped off the stem from the leaf.

'Batter up,' she said, holding the long stem like a baseball bat.

She swung at the oncoming bees, belting them back like Babe Ruth.

'Wow,' I muttered. 'You should think about a baseball scholarship for college.' She was Major League material.

'If we survive this,' she said.

Nesto crouched down, protecting himself as the bees bounced off his makeshift shield.

'We need to get out of here without letting any of these genetically modified zombees out into the open,' I announced.

'Agreed,' said Corina, grand-slamming a bee. 'But then what?'

'Tell someone, call the police,' I said.

'And tell them what? That you found a hive of super-insects that'll turn people into zombies . . . *just like you?*'

'We've got to warn people about what's going on here,' I said.

'Let's just get out of here first,' said Nesto. 'I don't want to be zombified. No offence, Adam.'

We ran across the field of mega-flowers looking for our original entrance, but got lost amid the massive magnolias and towering tulips.

Corina zoomed up into the air and floated down just as quickly. 'There are vents up there, but we won't fit through them. But I spotted a door. This way!'

We followed her to the edge of the greenhouse, but the steel door wouldn't budge. The bees were swarming above our heads and we were pinned against the magnetically sealed super-door.

'Can't you do anything?' called Corina as she swatted back the attackers.

There was nothing I could do and suddenly I felt pretty useless.

I hadn't thought about it until just then, with a swarm of angry zombees seeking to kill off my two best friends, that I really didn't have anything to offer. Nesto could turn into a powerful (albeit hungry) monster that could dig tunnels, throttle cattle and ruin perfectly manicured flower beds. Corina not only looked great in black leather, but she could fly.

What could I do?

I'd learned more about make-up and moisturising that I'd ever thought possible, but I had no superpowers to speak of. I didn't even have an urge to go on a cannibalistic rampage through town. What kind of zombie was I?

I worried that I didn't belong in our little creature crew and that Corina and Nesto would die because I was such a lame zombie.

That was it! Being *worried* was my superpower.

And now it was time to use it.

22

In Which I Discover My Superpower

Corina had been right, I was neurotic. I fretted, agonised and worried about things. About almost everything. And what was I just worrying about? That Ernesto and Corina could do things that I couldn't.

Corina could fly.

Fly? No good to us trapped in a greenhouse.

They could *hide* their conditions better than I could.

Hide? Nah, there was nowhere left to hide. We were on the bees' home turf, surrounded by giant flowers.

I thought of my mom's flowers at home, and worried if I should tell her that I'd discovered who'd been digging them up.

Dig?

For gold! That was it. Ernesto could dig tunnels

when he was all chupa-*rrific*. And we needed a tunnel as soon as chupaly possible.

'Nesto,' I called out over the buzz of the swarm. 'Are you sure you can't mutate on demand?'

'It's not a party trick, Adam,' he snapped.

Corina was hitting home runs but the zombees were getting more aggressive. 'We need you to go to that slimy place right now!' She couldn't hold the bees off forever.

'To dig a tunnel out of here!' I said. 'We need you!'

'I don't like going chupa,' he whined. 'You guys know that.'

'Pretty please!' Corina shouted, before turning to Nesto with a smile. 'With a chargrilled rat on top?'

Nesto licked his lips, tempted by the rodent for cherry replacement.

'Down is the only way out,' I urged. 'We need you on this one, Nest.'

He shuffled his feet and sighed. 'All right, but just don't look, okay?'

'No problem,' I said looking away, grabbing his leaf to shield him from the bees and me from the sight of an eleven-year-old sprouting scales.

'Any time now!' urged Corina, bunting a bee.

Nesto screeched. I made the mistake of looking. He was convulsing on the dirt, alternating between the foetal position and a snow angel without the snow. His smooth tweenage skin was transforming into slimy green scales as his dark brown eyes bulged into black lizard bulbs. It was one of the most disgusting things I'd ever seen.

And the most amazing. Nesto had wilfully transformed himself into a horrible monster to save his friends.

But his heroics came at a cost. As Ernesto writhed in the dirt, becoming the lizard-boy, his clothes slipped off in a filthy mess. He looked really upset.

'Don't worry, Ernesto, I've got stain remover for these,' I said, reassuring the transmutating lizard as I picked up his shirt and jeans. I think it helped because he looked up at me, in full chupa form and snarled his now trademark hiss-roar.

I'm pretty sure he was hissing, 'Thanks, Adam. You're a good friend.'

'You're welcome, Nesto,' I said. 'Now dig!'

Chupa-Nesto dug his front claws into the dirt, spraying Corina and I with soil as he frantically burrowed an escape tunnel.

He was so fast that suddenly he was hiss-roaring from the other side of the glass.

'Good thinking, Adam,' said Corina.

'Really?'

She swatted away two more angry bees. 'Yeah, maybe your brain isn't that decomposed after all.'

'Vegans first,' I insisted. I wasn't being polite, I was being scared. I really didn't want to burrow in the dirt.

Corina grabbed Nesto's clothes from me and dived for the tunnel. 'Hurry it up, Adam, or those bees'll bite you on the butt!'

I held Nesto's tulip leaf up, and a dozen zombees bounced off it before I held my breath and scrambled into the dirt. As soon as I was in, I turned over on my back and kicked at the roof of the tunnel, stopping the bees from following us in. I didn't want to take a chance that any bees might get loose in the open.

The collapsed tunnel was dark, dirty and very tight. For a moment, I was back in my grave. I felt stuck. I couldn't move. I was surrounded by the dirt, consumed by it. I felt alone and overwhelmed by the filth around me.

I moved myself on to my front, in a crawling

position and tried to edge forwards. But I couldn't. There was too much staining soil. I would never be clean again. I closed my eyes and wished it would all get washed away.

I heard Nesto laugh at the word 'butt' and relaxed a little. I reminded myself that I'd already climbed out of a grave. I could do this.

Don't think of it as dirt, I told myself. *Think of it as an opportunity for a bath.*

I moved my hands in front of me and shunted my knees forward.

I finally reached the light at the end of the tunnel and felt a cold hand. Corina gripped my left hand and Nesto's claw tightened around my right hand.

'Ooh-ah,' I winced. 'Easy on that finger bone.'

Together, they pulled me out. Once I emerged, I stood up and looked down at my clothes covered in soil.

'You're okay now, zom-boy,' said Corina, dusting me off.

As soon as I was out, Nesto backfilled the tunnel and I caught my reflection in the glass, filthy and probably covered in soil-borne diseases. But as the bees slammed into the zombee-proof glass, I felt triumphant that the three of us were safe and the zombees were contained.

Chupa-Nesto panted and howled as he mutated back to human form. He did a little dance, shaking out the last of the chupa from his system.

'Thanks, Nesto,' I said. 'And thanks, Corina, for flying us up and over Plante. I wish I had your powers.'

'You just keep using that Meltzer melon,' she said. 'And nice digging, lizard-lips.' I suppose those count as compliments in Transylvania. 'But puh-lease put some clothes on.'

Corina handed Nesto his clothes and he wriggled into his soiled tops and bottoms. I heard a *beep-beep-beep* as the gaming device slipped from Nesto's jeans pocket. I picked it up for him. 'Here you go, Nesto, you earned a play.'

But the little box wasn't for video games after all. It was a GPS. The screen showed a map of the university and a cluster of thousands of red dots in the greenhouse: the zombees.

'Guys,' I said. 'It's a tracking device. For the bees.' I zoomed out and saw that one red dot wasn't trapped with the others. One red dot was bouncing on the screen, on the far side of campus. 'And there's one missing.'

They looked at the screen and we all stared at the lone red dot in the outside world.

'That one's loose,' said Ernesto, finally catching his breath.

'Adam,' started Corina. 'Do you think . . .'

I was a step ahead of her. These angry bees were bigger than the uninvited guest at my birthday party, but I figured they'd had three months of Professor Plante's evil growth hormones to reach their unnatural size.

I tapped the red dot on the screen.

'I bet you anything that's the bee that killed me.'

Corina smiled. 'Party pack of Pop Rocks?'

23

In Which I Profess to Have Another Father

We followed the blinking red dot on the Bee-P-S device along a tree-lined campus boulevard. Classes were over for the week and the campus had a carnival atmosphere. The various clubs and activity groups of Croxton U were out in full force at something they called the 'Croxton Club Fair', attempting to recruit students into their ranks. The main campus boulevard was lined on both sides with tables representing every club or society under the sun – and some that had probably never seen the sun.

We were handed flyers by the unwashed Campus Crusade for Communism (annual membership thirty dollars), invited to join the Croxton Cleavers (the butchery club), and accosted by a gang of mimes washing invisible windows.

'This place is scary,' said Ernesto.

Corina looked around, unimpressed. 'These people are freakier than we are.'

I'd been coming to campus since I was little, so I took it all for granted. I'd sat quietly in the back of my dad's lecture halls while he'd bored undergraduates to sleep. I'd eaten in the dining halls (free ice cream!) and napped in the spare beds of the teaching hospital where my mom learned to be a doctor. This place was familiar to me, but understandably strange to my friends.

'This is the college experience,' I said, recounting something my dad used to say when I would tag along, carrying his papers to grade. 'It's basically Disney World for people on the brink of adulthood.'

A guy in a robe offered us a milky drink that I'm pretty sure wasn't milk and invited us to his 'club' to worship at the church of Dudeism.

'I don't want to grow up,' shuddered Nesto.

'These people need treatment,' said Corina, 'not clubs.'

We passed through the gauntlet of extracurricular activities unscathed, though I did notice that Nesto picked up a button proudly proclaiming him to be a member of the knitting club.

'So?' he asked. 'Needlework relaxes me, keeps the chupa at bay.'

Corina was strangely interested. 'Wonder if it works for vampirism?'

And I wondered if she was getting bloodthirsty after last night's tasting. 'Are you getting any, you know . . . cravings?'

'I have a bit of a taste for it again,' she whispered. 'I'd been off the juice since my Vein Day.'

Nesto stopped walking and confronted us about our hushed talk. 'Are you guys doing secrets already?'

'No,' I said. 'Just talking.'

'Woman stuff,' Corina said.

Nesto waved his hands in surrender. 'I don't wanna to know,' he said as he turned around and kept walking.

'Come on, guys,' I said. 'We're close. The bee is over there, somewhere.'

We arrived at the gates to the stadium, Croxton cathedral to pigskin*.

On weekends, the football stadium (still proudly

* In Croxton, ten times as many people go to football games than church.

177

sponsored by Moca-Cola) would pack in the gridiron fans, but this afternoon it was swarming with SMOOCH-heads. They descended on the gates like bees to a hive. But these hive-minded concertgoers had one thing we didn't have: tickets.

At the iron gates, hulking security guards were checking everyone's tickets, leaving us on the outside looking in. I took my bearings, plotting a way to penetrate the fortress of football. The stadium was actually comprised of four sets of bleachers on each side of the field. The western bleachers, immediately in front of us and dwarfing the other three, faced a portable amphitheatre opposite.

'Does anyone have any money for tickets?' asked Nesto.

'My mom said it's sold out,' I said.

'I could fly,' offered Corina.

'And I could dig,' added Nesto.

As much as I liked the idea of using superpowers to gatecrash the concert, I worried that we'd draw too much attention to ourselves in a place filled with camera phones. I had taken Corina's warning about government officials to heart. Flying and chupa-digging were a YouTube sensation just waiting to happen. My power, however, was invisible. It was up to me. I'd have to *worry* my way in.

I tried to project my anxiety on to the university, the stadium staff and the band. What would SMOOCH worry about?

Not selling tickets? Nope, they had a Croxton sell-out on their hands.

Looking like painted morons onstage? Not really, they seemed to relish in the idea.

Their fan base dying off? Oddly not; there were just as many young people streaming into the stadium as ancients like my parents. SMOOCH was a multi-generational phenomenon. Like obesity.

What about their own *mortality?* Did the rockers worry about their own ticking clocks?

Mortality.

Death.

Zombies.

Ghosts.

Halloween.

Skeletons.

Hmmm, skeletons. In the grave . . . or in the closet?

Yes! These heavy metal rockers would surely be worried about their past catching up to them.

'Let's go around back,' I said, 'to the band entrance.'

Corina cleared her throat. 'Note that we're not in the band.'

The one (and only) benefit to sharing DNA with Amanda is that her constant influx of boy-band fanzines had educated me on the finer arts of photo-bombing celebrities. I'd learned from the pages of *GossipLips* that the best place to meet a boy-band member was at the stage door.

'The band's entrance isn't just for bands,' I said. 'It's where groupies, super-fans, stalkers and illegitimate children hang out.'

My Amanda education was paying off; I was a walking Wikipedia of celebrity-stalking tips. I'd learned from the columns of *Rock'N'Soul* that aging rock stars all had kids they didn't know about showing up and causing all sorts of problems for their current (and often sixth) wife.

My neurons fired so fast it hurt. 'We're going to be the band's kids they never knew they had!'

'That's so idiotic,' said Corina, 'that it might just work.'

We walked the perimeter of the fence until we found ourselves in the mammoth parking lot around the back. The performer's entrance was guarded by a bulging rent-a-cop spilling over his stool. His name tag read 'Gregor'.

'Wrong door,' Gregor grunted without looking up from his well-read copy of *GossipLips*.

'My sister reads that magazine,' I said.

Gregor folded it and shoved it down his behind – somewhere not even a third-rate gossip rag should be condemned to go.

'Oh, ah, yeah,' he stuttered. 'I read it for the crosswords.'

Corina stepped up and put on a woeful, lost puppy look and said, 'I read it to look at pictures of Johnny Falcon . . . my dad.'

'The lead singer of SMOOCH is your *father*?'

'Only he doesn't know it,' she said. She then put her arm around me and added, 'and this is my brother. From another mother.'

Brother?

Why not boyfriend?

I could've been her boyfriend, here to support her as she confronted her errant rock dad.

'Uh huh,' said Gregor, spotting the scam. 'And who's the runt?'

I spoke first. 'That's Allen Supulva's illegitimate kid. His growth is stunted by the drugs Allen says he doesn't do.'

Gregor hoisted his mass off the stool and attempted to cross his arms over his man-boobs.

'Listen, kidlets,' he grunted. 'I don't know how you broke out of kindergarten, but why don't you run home to your real mommies and daddies and let me finish my crossword.'

'Um, nah,' said Corina, 'I think we'll just call the media and have a press conference about why the most successful costumed band on the planet isn't taking care of the children they leave in their wake.'

I was loving how Corina picked up my ball and was running with it. I had to really work at lying; but she was a born bluffer.

Suddenly, Nesto burst into tears, joining the fray. 'I just want my daddy to know I exist,' he blubbered.

Wow, I thought. *I was surrounded by pros.*

'All we want is recognition,' stated Corina.

'Not money?' asked the guard.

Now it was my turn to pile on the deceit. I shook my head, looking serious and reflective. 'Our adopted fathers couldn't bear it. It's bad enough they're raising the demon seeds of rock devils. They couldn't take their money; their pride couldn't hack it.'

'I guess,' Gregor said, opening the barrier and waving us through. 'But if anyone asks, you didn't come this way.'

'Your incompetence is safe with us,' Corina said with a smile.

'It's perfectly normal,' he shouted after us. 'Three of every ten people cope with incontinence*, you know!'

'I know. I've got the pen,' I said.

As we walked along a long driveway that burrowed under the bleachers behind the amphitheatre, I couldn't quite believe that our ruse had worked. We'd woven together a lie worthy of the knitting club.

I felt like I'd earned a badge.

---

* I used to think incontinence meant a person without a continent, like boat people. But actually, it's just a big fancy word for peeing yourself. I've got a pen for an incontinent drug called Urinator and a mouse pad for a brand of adult-sized nappies called KatchAll.

24

In Which I Get Retarded

We walked surprisingly close to backstage before anyone stopped us, but two roadies blocked our path between the loading area and the stage. The pair looked like the 'before' in a TV makeover show. The female roadie wore a black tank top over her permatanned skin, showing off her bulging biceps. Her lanyard badge said her name was 'Melanie', but I wanted to scrawl 'Wash Me' on it like she was a dusty car. I was pretty sure her dreadlocks contained a bird's nest.

'Do I have to call security?' she growled, brandishing her clipboard like a weapon.

The male roadie, whose badge proclaimed him as 'Hecto', sported longer hippy hair than Melanie and a SMOOCH T-shirt over baggy cargo pants.

'Does she?' parroted Hecto the hippy.

Nesto took them literally. 'I don't know. Do you?'

'Don't be smart mouthed with me,' she snapped.

'His mouth isn't really that smart,' Corina clarified.

Nesto nodded. 'It's true. I'm still reading at a fourth-grade level.'

'Then what are you doing back here?' she barked. 'And don't tell me that you're illegitimate children of the band.'

'Ma-an,' drawled Hecto, 'we've had enough of them already. Every. Single. Town.'

I was hoping to continue with our fabulous fib, but instead I'd have to think fast on my feet. But Corina's feet were faster.

'We're here to sing the national anthem,' she announced.

'No, no, no,' Melanieoma replied.

Hecto glanced at her clipboard and informed us that, 'It's a group of retarded kids today.'

'Hector!' snapped Melanie.

'Hecto, yo,' he said. 'You know I dropped the R in protest against the Republican Party.'

'That's us,' Corina lied.

'Retards or Republicans?' asked Melanie. She immediately covered her mouth in embarrassed shock. 'Oh shoot!' she gasped. 'Am I allowed to say . . . *retards*?'

'I'm pretty offended,' I said, thinking of cousin Jimmy.

'Me too,' said Nesto, supportively, though under he breath he added, 'But not totally sure why.'

'Retarded, *adjective*, is okay,' I explained to everyone. 'Retard or retards, *noun*, is not.'

'It's just that you guys don't look . . .' Melanie said, desperately trying to defend her defamation. And then she looked straight at me. 'Well, he doesn't look normal.'

'He's clinically neurotic,' said Corina. 'I'm more Asperger's, and the runt here is well, we don't quite know what he is.'

The hippy dufus laughed. 'She said ass-burgers.'

'C'mon,' Corina said, pulling Nesto and I towards backstage. 'Let's go find that bee.'

Melanie cleared her throat. 'Hold up, you retards. You've got an anthem to sing.'

25

In Which I Meet My Killer

The ignorant roadies shuffled us towards something called 'the green room', which was neither green nor a room. It was a roped-off area backstage with a stained beige* sofa, two leather armchairs occupied by Dobermans, and a wooden coffee table holding a large glass bowl filled with green peanut Skedaddles.

'Dig in,' offered Melanie, 'I separated them myself.'

I didn't want any. Not just because of my peanut allergy, but because the grime under her fingernails suggested hands plus candy equalled food poisoning.

Corina shook her head. 'Vegan non-friendly! The shellac on the candy coating is actually made out of boiled cow's hooves. I'll pass.'

---

* The colour formerly known as white.

Nesto showed no such restraint. 'Where'd the other colours go?' he mumbled through a face full of Skedaddles.

'I sowed them in the field,' proclaimed Hecto. 'This time next year, that field'll be filled with Skedaddle trees. That's my gift to Crotchton.'

'It's Croxton,' I said. 'And thanks.'

'You're welcome, little chronically erotic man,' he said.

'Neurotic,' I clarified.

But he was in his own little world. 'Finally some recognition for my contribution. That field's like my legacy of this tour.'

Their radios blurted and Melanie and her candy farmer exited stage left to deal with a band crisis.

'You're on in ten,' she shouted back.

Corina kicked back on the sofa and put her pale hands behind her head. 'I could get used to the life of a rock star.'

'Well don't,' I said. 'We gotta find that bee.'

Nesto looked down at the GPS monitor and squealed. 'It found us!'

He pointed up. I gaped at the lighting rig high above us, suspending stage lights of every colour, and spotted something fluttering. At first I thought it was a bird, flapping from perch to perch atop the stage, but then I clocked its deadly colour combo – yellow and black. It was a bee the size of a pigeon.

And I swear it looked a lot like . . . me.

'Adam,' said Nesto, following my confused gaze. 'Does that bee have a *face*?'

'I . . . I . . . think so,' I stuttered.

'It sorta looks like an animated version of you,' said Corina. 'But like that ugly stop-motion kind, not the 3D computer-animated kind.'

I shot her a 'what are you talking about?' look. I'd never pegged Corina as an animation aficionado.

'Nesto does needlework, I do cartoons,' she explained. 'My therapist says animation keeps the cravings at bay. If I watch movies starring humans, I get, well, hungry. So I keep things animated and that keeps my blood lust in check. Except *Finding Nemo*. If I ever found him, I'd swallow him whole. He looks too tasty.'

'And the blue one,' added Nesto. 'She's funny and I bet yummy.'

As I walked to the rig ladder, I made a mental note that should I ever ask Corina to go see a movie, I'd make sure it was G-rated and not involving sea life.

'C'mon, guys,' I said, gripping the rungs. I briefly considered pausing to spritz the ladder rungs with sanitizer, but finding the bee was too important. Sometimes I surprise even myself.

One great thing about being technically dead is that my hands weren't at all sweaty. The steel ladder was all vertical, rising at least nine metres above the matte black stage, and in my living years I would've been perspiring like, well, like a guy climbing nine metres in the air without a net, harness or any other federally mandated safety equipment. But instead I was as smooth and dry as an antiperspirant ad. It felt good to be calm and collected. I rose steadily until I reached the rigging pipes.

From up here, I could see the entire stadium. The main bleachers facing the stage were filled with rows of made-up SMOOCH-heads. I quickly scanned the crowd, at least ten thousand strong, hoping to see my parents. But I couldn't pick out one painted-faced idiot from another.

The bee-boy was still there, perched above a red floodlight and looking at me quizzically. I opened my mouth to speak, and he matched my expression.

He tilted his head, his two antennae twitching in curiosity and confusion.

'Should we catch him?' called Corina from behind me.

I looked back to see her floating beside the lighting rig while Nesto deftly griped the pipes on all fours. He was poised like a tiger in a tree*. I guess his chupa-instincts weren't buried very deep below the surface.

The bird-sized zombee twitched, flitting his attention between Corina and myself. He looked scared and nervous. I always thought that I'd squish (and probably throw away the lethal shoe) the bee that killed me, but this mammoth bee not only looked frightened, but also looked too much like me to even think about squishing. Not to mention the gooey mess he'd make.

I've never had any interest in pets – I really didn't relish the idea of pooper-scooping after any animal. But looking at the zombee, I couldn't shake the feeling that I should protect him. I didn't understand how this

---

* My mom used to insist on trips to the Cincinnati zoo when I was younger until I finally put my foot down on the grounds that introducing these wild animals into urban areas could only lead to rampage.

creature could look like me; maybe our DNA fused when he stung me. This zombee was the product of strange science, but I felt a genuine connection with him, a type of instant kinship that only a resurrected zombie and genetically modified killer bee could share. I wouldn't say it was magical, but it was profound.

'I think he's okay,' I said to Corina. I looked at this mini Adam, this *Adamini* and promised: 'We're not going to hurt you, but I do want to know why you killed me.'

He buzzed excitedly and pointed his antennae out towards the crowd. It was trying to tell me something. At first I thought he was going to blame heavy metal music for his murderous behaviour, but then I saw it, beyond the throngs of painted faces, a white trailer truck storming into the parking lot.

'Nesto!' I called back. 'Hand me your binoculars.'

'Please,' he said.

'What?'

'You could say please, Adam.'

I knew I was feeling stressed if the chupa-runt was lecturing me on manners.

'Pretty please with a genetically modified, death-defying zombee on top.'

Nesto passed his plastic binos forward.

Luckily I had a spare packet of antibac wipes in my pocket. Of course, by now you know it wasn't luck; it was preparation. I quickly (but thoroughly) washed the viewfinders, held them to my eyes, and pointed the piñata-won binoculars at the approaching truck.

I saw Professor Plante get out of the cab and switch a lever on the side of the truck's trailer. The roof opened, releasing a cloud of large bees into the air.

Thousands of bees. *Zombees.*

And they were swarming straight for the stadium. For human trials.

26

In Which I Defile
the National Anthem

I have to admit, and I'm not proud of this, that my first instinct wasn't to warn everyone. As I watched the swarm of killer zombees fly towards the penned-in, unsuspecting crowd, I thought for a brief, unheroic moment: *at least I won't be on my own.*

If everyone in town went zom, then maybe I wouldn't have to hide who I really was. If zombies became the majority, then I wouldn't have to hide my greying skin and decomposing flesh behind MAC and long sleeves. But death was still death, and as much as I didn't want to be the odd zom out, I really didn't want my parents (and if I'm honest, even my sister) to die, come back and have to look like this. No, I didn't wish resurrection on anyone*.

---

* Except maybe Martin Luther King, JFK, and Jim Henson. It'd be great to have those guys back.

'We've got to warn them!' I declared.

Corina hovered in the air and grabbed Nesto and me. She pulled us from the rig and floated us down from the pipes toward centre stage. The crowd burst into cheers.

'You just outed yourself,' I shouted above the frenzy.

'As if,' she smirked as we touched down to thunderous applause. 'These fools are expecting showmanship!'

She was right. The crowd was hungry for a spectacle. They just thought we were a gimmick.

'They're clapping for us,' beamed Nesto. He took a bow, soaking up the praise.

But Corina burst his bubble. 'They're clapping for the special effects. Three retards flying in to sing the national anthem. Don't let it go to your head.'

I stepped to the front of the stage to warn the crowd of their impending apocalypse. 'There's a swarm of deadly bees coming to kill you all!'

But the crowd cheered on. Sure they were idiots, disinterested in their own impending demise, but I must admit that the sound of twenty thousand hands clapping felt pretty great. Offstage, Melanie caught my eye, holding up a clipboard that read: 'Anthum!'

I guessed they didn't teach spelling at roadie school.

Suddenly, two massive flags unfurled on either side of the stage. The crowd fell silent for the stars and stripes, putting their hands on their soon-to-be-unbeating hearts. I pointed to the sky above the stands, where the unseen bees were swarming.

'The killer bees are coming! They'll turn you all in to zombies like me. Look—'

Corina thrust a mic in my hand and I continued. '—can't you see!'

But they couldn't see. They wouldn't see. They just started singing along.

'*By the dawn's early light.*'

'You gotta sing, Adam,' said Nesto. 'It's like, the law.'

He had a point. America was the land of the free, where flag burning and not standing to attention at our national anthem were crimes of treason. All my pent up lip-synching finally bubbled to the surface. I let my vocal chords off their leash.

'*What so proudly we hailed at the twilight's last gleaming!*'

'You really can't sing,' winced Nesto.

'OhMyCount,' Corina cried, cupping her ears. 'Make it stop!'

The crowd kept singing, their patriotism shining through their aural anguish.

'*Whose broad stripes and bright stars,*' I continued, musically describing our nation's flag design.

I heard my first boo. And then I heard another one. *Was my voice really that bad?*

'Oh, perilous night!' complained Corina.

'You're butchering the anthem,' warned Nesto. 'I think it counts as treason.'

The crowd glared, booing me off the stage. I flashed back to Mr Ealson, our music teacher, condemning me to a middle school career of lip-synching and remembered the 'triple-threats' laughing at my awkward auditions. I recalled Dad urging me (begging me) to 'play to my strengths'. I felt defeated and ashamed. And in front of the largest crowd ever assembled in Croxton, I felt like a freak.

The booing was louder now. I looked up to avoid their death stares. Then I noticed that they weren't the only ones offended by my terrible singing. The zombees were hating it too.

One bee dropped out of the sky, dead. Then another. Then the rest of the bees buzzed backwards, spinning in circles, and smashing into one another. The swarm was in chaos. My treasonous singing was actually killing them. I may have been rupturing eardrums, but I was saving the day.

'*Through the perilous night!*' I sang with renewed enthusiasm. I powered through the rest of the anthem like I was opening the Super Bowl. At the end, the crowd cheered . . . out of relief.

'Never, ever sing again, Adam,' said Nesto. 'It hurts too much.'

'Never, ever stop,' said Corina, surprisingly supportive. 'Look! The zombees are regrouping.'

With my fatal voice silenced, the remaining swarm regrouped and started to descend on the stadium.

'Sing something else,' pleaded Nesto.

It was a fair request. I didn't think I should sing the anthem again, for fears that there was a special place in Guantanamo Bay for vocal terrorists like me. I had to think fast. It was a toss up between 'Oh Canada' (the only other anthem I knew) and show tunes. I decided to get even with Mr Ealson.

I went with show tunes.

27

In Which I Say Bye Bye Zombee

If my terrible singing voice was the key to stopping Croxton becoming overrun with zombies, then I'd sing terribly with gusto.

I clutched the microphone and chose 'Put On A Happy Face!' from *Bye Bye Birdie*. Adam Meltzer was going to be heard!

Freed from the scornful looks of my music teacher, I sang loud and I sang proud. I had so much song in me that I probably didn't even need the microphone (which I kept at minimum safe distance from my mouth since countless rock stars sang and spat into it) but I used it to amplify my life-saving vocals.

I looked across a sea of heavily made-up faces grimacing while I sang. The audience was wincing in pain, booing and jeering, but I didn't dare stop because above them, the zombees were retreating again.

Nesto held his ears and doubled over while Corina made a break for it.

I was counting on the moral support of both my freakish friends, but I suppose a solo is called a solo for a reason. I was in the spotlight, alone. Just me, and my voice. This was my moment – my time to shine, even if it meant showing everyone how tone deaf I truly was. It was my solo. But suddenly, I heard myself in echo.

Corina returned to centre stage and tugged on my sleeve. 'You can stop now!'

I pointed up to the retreating swarm of zombees and kept singing, keen to stave off the attack.

'I got those roadies to loop your voice through the speakers,' she said. 'You can stop singing, please! The recording is making a vocal shield over the whole stadium.'

And with that, my way-off-Broadway debut crashed to a halt. I stopped putting on a happy face and took a slight bow. It was well timed, because I felt the whoosh of a tomato fly over my head. As the projectile fruit* soared over me, I wondered: what kind of person brings a tomato to a concert?

---

* Yes, it's a fruit. Most people think that tomatoes are vegetables, but those same people probably think that crisps count as vegetables too.

I mean, did he hope that the performance would be so bad that he'd be the one to throw the first tomato? Or was he simply prepared with a juicy treat and took the opportunity to throw it? Sure, it's a healthy snack, but apples and pears are the more portable fruits. How did he transport that tomato? Surely not in his pocket, where it would squish, leak and ooze (vitamin-filled) tomato juice down his pants, leaving not only an uncomfortable wet patch on his leg but also a stubborn stain.

So many questions and so little time to ask security for a CCTV replay of the tomato toss and track down the pitcher for answers.

I rose from my fruit-dodging bow and listened to my recorded voice as it rang out through the stadium. Hearing it broadcast over the speakers, I heard my voice as others hear me. I suppose Atticus Finch was right, and I'm paraphrasing here: you never truly know a person until you listen through their ears.

In my own head (and in the shower), my voice sounded smooth and melodic. But aloud, replayed through the magic of recording technology, it sounded like cats in a . . . well, you know.

I had to accept that my voice was awful. But

mourning my vocal abilities would have to wait. I still had a horde of would-be zombie-making bees to stop.

'Guys, we've got to lead those bees back to their greenhouse,' I announced. 'Contain them!'

'You're not exactly the pied piper,' said Corina.

'I know, I get it. I'm not Pavarotti. But if they won't follow me, maybe they'll follow one of their own.'

I looked at my Adamini bumbleganger, perched on the drum kit behind us. The zombee widened his eyes as I approached him.

'Hey, little fella, I need your help,' I said, not knowing if the bee-boy hybrid understood what I was saying. But he nodded and so I continued. 'Can you lead the bees back to the greenhouse?'

His antennae twitched. He shook his little black furry head. I knew that look: fear. He understood all right, but he was scared. I decided to play to his vanity instead of his sense of service.

'If those bees stay loose, they'll turn all of these people into zombies and all of them into, well, creatures like you. You're unique now. You're special. But if they attack, then you'll be just like every-bee else. Is that what you want?'

He shook his head again and he huffed. I knew that look too: ego.

He buzzed his wings and hovered into the air, ready to fly.

'We'll follow you,' I promised, 'but you need to lead those bees back to the hive.'

Corina looked skeptical. 'Can we really rely on that monster?'

'Look at us,' I said. 'We're all monsters. And if we can't rely on each other, then what's the point? We're different from everyone else; we've got to stick together.'

'Thought you didn't want to be different?' asked Nesto.

'I am who I am. I can't change that. And you know what, I like being a zom-boy. And I like our little freak-show club. We may be undead, mutated or have unresolved eating issues, but we're unique and we're together. So let's work together to save this town.'

Corina nodded. 'Good speech, Adam. I'm in.'

'Me too,' said Nesto. 'Let's go!'

I led them backstage, past the confused-looking roadies and past the four living corpses that comprised SMOOCH.

We found the exit and ran through the parking lot to the north side of the university grounds.

'We'll cut through the fields,' I said. The campus was bordered by cornfields to the north and instead of navigating the campus club fair, I'd take a short cut through the fields to the greenhouses. But halfway across the parking lot, the most awful thing happened.

I needed to poo.

28

In Which I Face the PortaPotty

I froze on a faded yellow line in the parking lot. My body seized up and I couldn't take another step. My bowels rumbled and I knew I was in in trouble.

Nesto and Corina kept running until they finally noticed I wasn't keeping up. Time slowed down. I saw the swarm of zombees retreating to the greenhouses. I heard the roar of the crowd as SMOOCH took to the stage. I felt the warm Ohio breeze sweep playfully through my softened hair, and I inhaled a fart smell so foul that it could only be generated by a once-dead digestive system.

Nesto and Corina stopped and stared. Nesto ran back to grab me. I warned him, but it was too late.

'I wouldn't come too—' was as far as I got before Nesto cupped his nose and fell to the asphalt.

'It burns!' he yelped as he writhed in parking spot 1583.

'What's going on?' asked Corina.

'Stay there!' I warned. I really didn't want her to think of me as some kind of zombie stink bomb. It was bad enough she'd heard me singing and was grossed out my physique. I'd lost her two of our five senses and didn't want to add smell to the blacklist.

'My nose,' cried Nesto.

'Get up, you big baby,' ordered Corina.

'Smell is a chupacabra's dominant sense,' he complained. 'And Adam's butt just handicapped me.'

'Nesto, get up. And Adam, move your butt!'

But I couldn't move. Not without awakening the slumbering faeces within.

'Corina, I really have to go.'

'I know, c'mon, those zombees are getting the jump on us. And we don't want to leave your little zombee hanging!'

'Not that,' I said, 'I really need the little zombie's room . . . right now.'

'You've got to be kidding? Can't you hold it?'

'I've been holding it for over three months. It's happening now.'

There was no way I could make it back into the stadium. Not that I'd want to use a toilet frequented by thousands of people anyway. But nor did I want to drop anchor on the sizzling asphalt of the parking lot in front of my monster crew. I tensed my body from the inside out and scanned the horizon for options.

I looked to the cornfields bordering the parking lot. I could find privacy amid the tall cornstalks but I'd be defecating on our food supply. What if that poo-fertilized corn found its way to my dinner plate? I couldn't take that risk.

And then I spotted it, the plastic box of my salvation and my repulsion. The upright blue rectangle stood at the far edge of the parking lot, beside a stationary digger and an unrolling steamroller. The small construction site must've been set up to repave the parking lot, but right now it was my best option for a secluded sit-down.

I took one step and regretted it. I was in serious danger of defacing my NinjaMan underwear.

'What's your problem?' asked Corina.

'He can't move,' explained Nesto. 'It's probably touching the cloth.'

'OhMyCount,' gagged Corina. 'Boys are disgusting.'

I nodded furiously, trying not to move any muscles lower than my neck. I felt helpless, like a poo-filled piñata waiting to burst. Nesto looked me right in the eye and said, 'I've got this.'

He gently grabbed my left elbow and waved Corina over to grab my right one.

'Adam, just keep your arms tucked in and we'll lift you all the way,' he said. 'Just don't move your legs.'

I rose above the (not yet repaved) road only a centimetre or two, but it was enough. My two friends carried me across the parking lot as I tensed my arms close to my chest and closed my eyes. I focused all of my energy inwards, keeping my poo from making an early debut.

As I got closer to the blue PortaPotty, I felt the panic rise.

I couldn't go in there.

Maybe cornfield or parking-lot pooping wasn't so bad after all? At least those options were out in the open; in the fresh air. As my friends placed me at the door to the PortaPotty, I smelled the faint stench of the deposits left by construction workers.

I had no choice. It was now or . . .

No, it was now.

I lurched forward like a tweenage Frankenstein, knees straight and careful not to bounce as I lumbered. I reached out for the blue door to Hell.

I grabbed the bottom of my shirt and used it as a glove as I pulled open the plastic door, unleashing an unholy stench of digested doughnuts.

Unlike another blue box I knew, this portable potty was no TARDIS*. Come to think of it, where did the Doctor relieve himself? But any questions I had for quirky British science fiction were immediately swept away by the invasion of thousands of poo particles attacking my nose.

I surveyed the off-white toilet seat and cursed myself for my lack of preparedness. Ordinarily, if I wasn't hunting death-defying bees and trying to solve the mystery of my own murder, I'd have packed sanitary toilet seat covers, industrial strength hand solvent, and a surgical mask pre-soaked in Febreze**. But some things you just can't plan for.

I suddenly felt very alone inside the blue poo prison. The last time I felt this alone was in another rectangular confinement: my coffin. *At least I'm not dead*, I told myself. *Well, at least I'm not dead-dead.* While part of me – my nose – thought that real death might be a preferred option at this moment, I knew I was lucky not to be in my final resting place.

I held my breath, dropped my pants and undies, hovered my butt over the hole, and pooed like I was living.

And you know what?

I felt alive again.

29

In Which I Lose My Grip

I burst from the PortaPotty energised and a whole lot lighter. I had stared down a (very sensible) fear, conquered it, and left my mark for good measure. Maybe it was the beginning of the new me. Maybe. I'd done it. It was in the past; which was a great place for it. Now, it was time to move on. And sterilize my hands.

'Why are you smiling, zom-boy?' asked Corina.

'Feels good, donnit?' said Nesto.

'Thanks for your help, guys,' I said. 'I couldn't have done that without you.'

'You make it sound like we wiped,' snarked Corina.

'Jeez, Corina,' I said, 'just take the praise.'

''Kay,' she said. 'Well done! You used a potty! You're ready for kindergarten.'

I ignored her sarcasm and rummaged through my backpack for my hand gel. I squeezed a generous dollop of sanitizer, thoroughly lathered, and inhaled the sweet scent of evaporating alcohol. My nose was happy again, and I was relieved, sanitized, and ready.

To save the world.

We cut through the cornfields towards the greenhouse. The zombees were swarming through the glass and I spotted Adamini corralling the swarm like an airborne sheep dog.

'He's doing it!' Nesto shouted.

'C'mon,' I urged. 'We've got to seal them in.'

Corina flew us over the fence and we found our original *Great Escape** tunnel. I looked at Nesto and didn't even need to ask. He strained and suddenly sprouted claws and scales, but only on his arms. The rest of him was still human.

'Wow, Nesto,' I gasped. 'You're really controlling it.'

He smiled a fang-free, eleven-year-old boy smile. I think he was pretty proud of himself. Nesto burrowed in and I sucked up my apprehensions and followed straight after. There was a time for cleaning and a time for mess. And this mission was getting messy.

---

* My dad's favourite movie. About a group of prisoners of war who plan and carry out a (SPOILER ALERT!!!) doomed escape from a POW camp.

'Way to get filthy, Adam!' said Corina, as she emerged from the tunnel.

It felt like we were a team, all using our powers for good. I wondered if this was how NinjaMan felt all the time. As I led my friends through the giant flowers to the door to the subterranean level, I fantasized about a series of comic books about me. Suddenly, I saw everything framed in rectangular storyboard boxes.

'But do you actually have a plan?' Corina asked in a speech bubble. 'Or are you just going to ask the zombees to lie down and play dead?'

The thought bubble over my head read: *She's mean to me because she likes me.*

But that had to wait. I did have a plan: it was time to lock down these zombees. I rushed down the steel steps, two at a time, to the secret lower level and waited for all the deadly zombees to collect inside.

Adamini flew to the glass and smiled proudly. He'd done it. He'd led all the killer bees away from the crowd and back to their glassed-in hive.

Corina grabbed a remote control from the wall; it looked like a garage-door opener. She pressed a button and the grates above the swarming hive began to tilt shut.

'Get out of there!' I shouted to Adamini.

I pointed up to the grates, urging him to fly to safety before Corina sealed the swarm in. But he didn't flee. He kept flying around the chamber, luring the other bees inside. He was their pied piper and the bees would surely follow him.

'You have to let him go, Adam,' said Corina. 'He's done his job.'

The metal grates above their chamber sealed shut in sync, like ten horizontal garage doors closing in unison. They were trapped. And they knew it. I couldn't risk the swarm escaping, and my little zombee knew it too, but that didn't mean he'd have to stay trapped with the rest of them.

'They look pretty peeved,' said Nesto.

The bees zoomed and darted around Adamini, buzzing and nipping at him. He'd led them into a trap, and they were furious. He didn't stand a chance against this angry swarm. He looked at me, helpless and resigned.

I had to get him out.

I opened the outer glass door to the vestibule between the lab and the chamber. I stepped into the glass box and pulled the outer door shut behind me.

I opened the inner door and stepped into a deafening sound of buzzing.

'C'mon!' I yelled, holding out my arms for my zombee-double to fly into. He darted up, encircled me, and then landed in my arms like a football. *So that's what catching a pigskin feels like*, I thought. I suddenly saw why Brock and the football team were so excited about their on-field antics, it felt pretty great.

Adamini's little (though huge for a bee) body was itchy and twitchy. I scooped him close to me with my left hand as the pulsating mass of angry bees swarmed towards me. I turned for the door, reaching for escape with my right arm.

And that's when it came clean off.

30

In Which I Confront the Queen

My newly independent arm kept its grip on the door for a moment before falling to the muddy ground. I suppressed the urge to scream and stood in shock. It wasn't like I'd never seen blood before. I'd had numerous nosebleeds. Once I punctured my eyebrow with the broken handle of a vacuum-cleaner attachment while toasting dust bunnies under my bed, so I wasn't a complete stranger to my own platelets. But zombie blood was different.

I looked down at my right shoulder where my arm used to attach. The fabric of my distressed long-sleeved vintage tee was severed and the hole was a bloody mess. But instead of flowing a vibrant red, this blood was viscous, dark crimson. It looked like rotten jam oozing from my open armpit. I knew my body was different now, but this was the first time I'd witnessed the blood of the undead.

'Watch out!' called a tinny-sounding Corina through a speaker in the wall. 'Behind you!'

Her urgent voice rang out through the chamber above the buzzing. I turned around to face two reflective black eyes: a bee at least twice the size of Adamini. Hovering in the air, this owl-sized beast of an insect must've been the queen bee. Her buzz was like a roar, drowning out the hive. She swung a leg at my head and I ducked just in time.

She'd severed my arm and was hoping to slice off my head.

I knew from the Hamberger that bees had a strong hierarchy to their hive. She was in charge and she was going to prove it to me in front of her worker zombees. The queen bee moved herself between me and the door, trapping me in. She wasn't done with me yet.

'I'm not giving up any more body parts,' I said.

She buzzed a high-pitched squeal of a buzz; an attack cry. Queenie flapped her wings into a blur and hovered in the air, right above me. Her legs were like knives and she sliced at me again. I rolled out of the way, still clutching Adamini, but she sliced again, lightning fast.

I couldn't keep this up for long. She was a razor-sharp mutant bee bent on revenge and I was a one-armed zombie worrying about getting dirt in my wound. It was hardly a fair fight.

She picked me up with two of her legs and threw me across the chamber. It sounded like the hive was actually laughing at me. I hit the ground hard and lost hold of Adamini. He slipped out of my grip and rolled loose. I rose to grab him but the queen bee pounced, slamming into me and knocking me back down.

It was zombee 1, zombie 0.

She dragged me to the back of the chamber and dropped me on to an icky, sticky honeycomb that gripped my clothes and skin, holding me down. I was stuck.

I expected the queen to finish me off right then, perhaps slicing and dicing me with her razor-sharp legs. I wondered if, in my zombie form, I'd survive being cut into pieces, perhaps becoming just a talking head rolling around. I was lost in my own paranoid fantasy when Corina's voice snapped me out of my daymare.

'Buzz off!'

I pried my head up from the sticky honey to see Corina hovering in the air and Nesto, in full chupacabra form, hiss-roaring on all fours.

'If anyone's going to chop up Adam and throw him on to honeycomb,' growled Nesto, 'it's us!'

'Thanks, Nesto. I think.'

The queen sliced at Corina, but the vegan vampire was faster than the super-bee. Corina give the queen a roundhouse kick, sending her reeling. But the giant bee recovered and attacked again.

'Hey, Adam,' snorted Nesto. 'Look, girl fight!'

I struggled to raise my head. 'Just get me off this thing.'

Nesto shredded the honeycomb into a sweet-smelling powder. I rose to my feet (at least I still had two) and spotted Corina in the air, fending off the queen's razor-sharp legs.

They tussled in the air, over and over like a load of laundry.

'Pull at her antennae, Corina!' I called, remembering what the Hamberger said about bees' sense of direction. 'It'll disorientate her!'

Corina flipped in the air, landed on the queen's back and tied the bee's antennae in a knot. The queen lurched and buzzed uncontrollably, slamming herself into the glass wall between the chamber and lab. Corina smashed into the glass, upside down, and slumped to the floor.

Nesto and I rushed to Corina and helped her up.

'How'd you know that?'

'I pay attention in class,' I said. I spotted Adamini and picked him up with my one functional arm. He squealed when he spied chupa-Nesto.

'Don't worry,' I reassured the zombee, 'he's with us.'

The mega-queen twitched on the ground. She was angry, confused and unable to fly. She swung her legs wildly, tripping and falling as she sliced at the air. Furious and disoriented, the queen bee stared at me.

'Your zombie-making days are over,' I told her.

'And you're ugly too,' hissed Nesto, still in his hideous chupa-mode.

Corina kicked the queen bee like a soccer ball. 'You mess with one of us,' she said, 'you mess with all of us.'

The bee bounced off the wall, and swirled in the dirt.

'And I don't like mess,' I added.

The queen bee flailed on the ground, unable to strike back. Corina's sailor knot had knocked out her senses. I looked down at Adamini and told him, 'She can't hurt you any more.'

'But they can,' said Nesto, pointing his scaly tail. 'Look.'

I turned around. The entire hive was swarming towards us. The worker bees were flying in fast, looking to avenge their dethroned queen.

I rushed for the door. 'Let's go!'

Corinia flew and Nesto leaped as I led the way into the glass chamber between the two rooms. Corina sealed the inner door shut and the buzzing was suddenly fainter.

'I got you a souvenir, zom-boy,' said Corina.

She tried to plop my lifeless arm between my zombee and chest, but little Adamini was grossed out by the limb. He buzzed and flew up to my shoulder, allowing me to grasp by own dismembered arm. It was good to be reunited with my limb, but I had no idea if it was even possible to reattach it. I remembered once that Amanda had taken all the arms and legs off of my NinjaMan action figures (including the limited-edition Hawaiian Surf-Attack figure)

221

and I spent a painstaking week matching limbs to bodies; snapping them back together. But real life wasn't like Made in China plastic. In real life, I was a zombie with coagulated blood and a missing arm. I was facing an armless eternity.

I thought of all of the things I'd never accomplish. I'd never pitch in the Majors. I'd never arm wrestle. I'd never ride a hog cross-country in search of trouble. I'd never audition for Cirque du Soleil. The life that I'd never lead flashed before my slate grey eyes. But I realised that I didn't really want to do any of those things. My life was in Croxton, with my new friends. So I simply said, 'Thanks Corina.'

'Glad to give you a hand.'

Nesto laughed as she pushed open the outer door, spilling us into the lab.

'You've been dying to say that, haven't you?' I asked.

'Pretty much the only reason I picked up your spare part,' she admitted.

'Fair enough,' I said. 'I don't think I could bring myself to handle one of your torn-off limbs.'

'Like I'd let you.'

'Right. Anyway, thanks again and thanks for coming to my rescue.'

'What are friends for?' she asked.

It was a fair question, and got me thinking. 'Well, I suppose the original purpose of friends was to broaden the survival chances of tribal clans beyond the core family unit and—'

'It was a rhetorical question,' Corina said with slight shake of her head.

Nesto howled with laughter. 'Still sounds like rectum!'

'I'm glad I amuse you, lizard-lips,' she said.

'What are friends for,' I said. 'Right?'

'Tribal survival,' quipped Corina, pointing to the glass. 'And I bet queen bee wishes she had more friends in hive places.'

In the chamber, the swarm of bees surrounded their queen. She disappeared in a cloud of black and yellow, completely enveloped by a mass of swirling insects.

'G-r-oss,' I wretched. 'Are they . . . eating her?'

'That is disgusting,' agreed Nesto in mid-transmutation. His skin was scaly and his hair drenched with sweat, or some kind of greenish chupa-gel. And his clothes were shredded from one too many mutation.

'You're one to talk,' said Corina.

I spotted a spare white lab coat on a hook and held it open for Nesto, now upright and enrobing himself in Mad Scientist White. 'That's better,' I said, buttoning up two of the coat's buttons.

'They *are* eating her,' Nesto said, looking through the glass.

'That's actually pretty consistent with vampire culture,' Corina said. 'We eat our leaders when they're no good to us any more.'

'Sick,' I said.

'But effective,' she said. 'And then we hold a banquet to feast on the body. Followed by a ball. It's all very refined and I get to wear heels.'

'I don't understand you people,' I confessed.

'Vampires or girls?' she asked.

'They're both just as strange,' I admitted.

'And scary,' said Nesto.

'C'mon, boys,' Corina laughed. 'Lets get us some Pop Rocks.'

'Ooh, yeah,' said Nesto, fully human and swimming in his borrowed* lab coat.

---

* Though I doubt he had any intention of returning it.

But suddenly, the hive chamber burst into flames.

'I didn't do it!' snapped Nesto. Clearly his instinctive response to any calamity.

'*Non*, but *moi* did!' said Professor Plante in his SMOOCH make-up, standing by his computer next to Dr Austin. 'And you are next.'

31

In Which I Stand Up to My Dad's Enemy

Dr Austin stared through me with a dismissive, slightly disgusted look adults usually reserve for nose-pickers and door-to-door salesmen. 'Think you're pretty clever, Meltzer?'

My invitation from MENSA may have been lost in the mail, but I was no dummy. I knew what side of the bell curve I landed on. 'As measured by standardised tests, yes, I think—'

'It's a rhetorical question,' said Corina again.

Nesto burst out laughing again, uncontrollably.

'Rhett-Tor-I-Cal,' I said, spelling it out. 'It doesn't even sound like rectum.'

'Made you say it, though,' he giggled.

Plante tapped another key on the computer and the fire in the chamber extinguished with a poof. The hive chamber was empty of bees but filled with smoke. He'd incinerated the entire hive with a click of the keys.

'You . . . killed . . . them all,' I stuttered, clutching Adamini close.

'A failed experiment,' said Austin. 'It's the scientific way. There is no progress without sacrifice.'

'And we love zee progress,' added Plante. 'We live for zee progress. And you will die for zee progress.'

'Hand that *thing* over, Meltzer,' ordered Austin, 'that remnant of a failed experiment; and I'll let you walk away.'

Adamini looked up at me from my shoulder. He was in my care and I wasn't going to let two deranged scientists burn him alive.

'*Non, non!*' protested Plante. 'We must kill them first. They have witnessed too much.'

'I might run for Senate, you imbecile,' said Austin. 'I'm not killing anyone. No one's going to believe these kids anyway. We just need to clean up this mess and get back to the business of progress.'

But I wasn't buying it. 'Progress like turning ten thousand SMOOCH heads into zombies?'

There was something else going on here in the bowels of Croxton University, something evil. I didn't know what Austin's master plan was, but I knew it stunk worse than a PortaPotty.

'Their musical preferences already make them half-dead,' Dr Austin said.

Plante shot his boss an outraged look and I spotted a division, a rupture in their relationship that I could exploit.

'He really doesn't think much of your favourite band,' I said.

'Band?' scoffed Dr Austin. 'Bunch of freaks in make-up.'

'Musical geniuses unappreciated by the mainstream,' argued Plante.

'You know professor, my dad's a big SMOOCH fan. And he says that Dr Austin was always bad mouthing people who like SMOOCH. I think that's why my dad and him aren't friends any more. What did he call you earlier, an imbecile?'

I could see Plante's cogs turning behind the make-up. But Austin wasn't listening. He stroked his beard and examined me, pulling down his glasses. He stared at me, focusing on my dismembered limb. 'So that's how you're back, Meltzer. You're back from the dead, not back from the feds.'

'Adam, he knows,' whispered Corina. 'Let's get out of here.'

Dr Austin examined the limb I was holding and laughed. 'So it did work. You are the proof I need. A human trial.'

'Let's go,' urged Corina.

Dr Austin examined me closely. 'Fascinating. The bee adopted your DNA when it stung you. I hypothesise that the process can be reversed.'

'What?' I asked.

'Adam,' urged Corina, tugging at my intact arm.

Dr Austin smiled. 'I can fix you, Adam. Like you were before.'

'You can?'

'He's lying!' cried Corina.

'You're the proof that death can be beaten,' he said. 'And my hypothesis states that death can be fully reversed with the right dosage of your DNA from that . . . from that creature.'

'You can make me normal again?' I asked.

'Yes, Adam. You don't have to be a freak. You can go back to just being a weird kid with a loser father. Hand over that thing and I'll set it all right.'

'Really?' I wondered.

'Adam,' said Corina, 'you were never *normal*.'

'So why be now?' asked Nesto.

I looked at my friends. On the outside, they both could pass for normal, but inside they weren't even close. And what was normal, anyway?

Being like everyone else?

Boring.

'She's right. I've never been normal and I like being a freak. Anyway,' I said, gesturing to my friends, 'I'm in good company.'

'Have it your way,' said Austin. For a brief moment, I thought, *great*. My way was to simply march up the steps, walk home, and get in trouble from my parents for ruining their concert and maybe have a bite of dinner while catching up on *Doctor Who*. But Austin had other ideas.

'Plante, do your worst!'

So much for Dr Austin's political ambitions.

The spindly professor charged, with a look of rage in his eyes. As he stepped closer, I noticed that tears were streaking down his red, white and black make-up.

'*Merci*, little meddler,' he sobbed. 'For I am a freak too!'

Suddenly, he stopped between Austin and me. The deranged and clearly repressed French scientist picked up his boss and threw him over his shoulder.

'Put me down, you imbecile!' yelled Dr Austin.

Plante carried the protesting president into the still smoldering chamber and threw him on to the charred ground. As Plante locked his boss behind the glass, Austin banged on the window and shouted silently. We couldn't hear him through the thick glass, but he was clearly pleading for his life.

'Um, you're not going to burn him alive are you?' I asked. I just wanted to be sure I wasn't inadvertently being party to more than one gruesome death this week.

'*Non*,' Plante replied, not fully convincingly. 'I don't think so.'

Then I had an idea. 'Well, if you really want to punish him . . . I mean teach him to appreciate your fine taste in music, why don't you pipe in all of SMOOCH's albums?'

'*Bon idée, petit* zombie!'

Plante busied himself at his computer, pulling up an epic playlist of mind-melting heavy metal and broadcasted it into the chamber. Behind the glass, Dr Austin cupped his ears and fell to his knees. He'd be begging for mercy and forgiveness by the time the first song was over.

I eyed the stairs, noting the steel door was ajar*. 'Let's exit stage *up*,' I whispered to my creature crew.

'Before he puts us in there,' Corina said.

'It's actually not so bad,' said Nesto, bobbing his head to the thrash metal.

We crept towards the steps, behind Plante's back as he watched his boss writhe in pain. But then he turned to catch us.

'Where do you think you're going?'

Nesto pointed. 'We're leaving because this place is creepy and our parents are probably wondering where we are.'

I caught Corina sigh under her breath, 'Like mine care.'

'Are we good?' I asked Plante. 'Should I worry?'

Plante smiled. 'Tell no one of this place and I'll keep your zombie secret.'

'Deal,' I said. 'But can I ask you a question?'

'You just did.'

---

* Again, not actually a jar.

He had me on a technicality there. 'Okay, can I ask you another question?'

'You just did, again.'

Corina shoved me.

'What are you guys doing down here with your weird experiments and death-defying zombees?'

'Our sponsor is the military,' Plante admitted. 'Our experiments are to keep soldiers alive . . . even if they're dead. The bees were a delivery for the serum.'

'An army of zombies,' I gasped.

'And I know they'd like to get their hands on you,' he threatened. 'So let us continue our work and you may live your afterlife.'

I nodded. We'd achieved a truce, for now. I led my friends up the stairs and into the greenhouse. We found our tunnel, made our great escape, and traipsed across campus.

As we walked back across university, the sounds of SMOOCH filled the air. Not from Plante's playlist, but from the stadium. The crowd cheered wildly. They'd clearly recovered from my performance and were getting the entertainment they'd almost died for.

'They have no idea how close they came today,'

I said. Adamini fluttered his wings and buzzed around us in the cool night air.

'It's better that they don't know,' said Corina.

Nesto sighed. 'Yeah, but a *graçias* would be kinda nice.'

'NinjaMan doesn't get any thanks,' I said. 'And he doesn't expect any either.'

'So, are we superheroes?' asked Nesto.

'Today we were,' said Corina.

She was right. *Today we were*.

And aside from losing an arm and uncovering an evil plot to kill off my town, I felt fantastic. In fact, I'm not sure I'd ever felt this good while I was alive. We'd saved everyone and we'd done it together.

It was the weirdest week of my life, the first of my afterlife; but by far the best. I didn't know what lay ahead for a young zombie like me. I got stung by a bee, died, came back a few months later and now I had my whole afterlife ahead of me.

But I'd worry about that later.

32

In Which I Vow to Fight Evil

I arrived home to an empty house and popped my loose arm in the freezer beside Dad's secret stash of bacon. I'd missed dinner so I single-handedly made myself an avocado sandwich on decrusted toast*.

It turned out that little Adamini shared more than my looks, he also had a soft spot for avocado on toast. It was nice to enjoy a meal in peace without Amanda's inane chatter about boys or Dad's loathing about his career nose-dive or Mom asking me about my poo (though this time I did have something substantial to report); but I did miss them as I sat alone at the table.

---

*   Two (2) pieces of lightly toasted rye bread, crusts removed and discarded. One (1) organic avocado peeled and sliced into ten (10) slices, evenly placed on the bread. One (1) vine-ripened tomato roughly chopped, placed around the curves of the avocado. Fresh watercress generously sprinkled throughout and then topped with extra virgin garlic olive oil.

They could have died tonight, and I'm glad my creature crew saved them zombiedom. I had a hunch we'd be called on again to save the day. The three of us, four if you count Adamini, stumbled on to the tip of the weirdness iceberg below Croxton. I was sure our run-in with the zombees wasn't going to our last encounter of the crazy kind.

I got to wondering – a vampire, a chupacabra, and now a zombie – what else was going on in Croxton? And who else might need our help?

After dinner, washed down with watered-down orange juice, and completed with one of my dad's homemade brownies (nut free, gluten free, but full of cocoa), I went to the computer in Mom's office. I carefully disinfected the keyboard with Spraysol and created a blog. I decided that Nesto, Corina, and I were just like superheroes, and there might be people out there who'd need our help.

As Adamini nested atop Mom's bookcase of medical journals, I set up www.adammeltzer.com and offered our services to the world (well, to the town, and certain parts of the tri-state area if Mom or Dad didn't mind driving):

If you have a problem with the unnatural or just plain

weird that needs solving, and provided that I don't have homework, I'll do my best to investigate. Note that I do not do babysitting, yard work or dog walking. Just leave a comment below and I'll get back to you.

I was wrestling with Wordpress when the parentals arrived home belting out highlights from the SMOOCH show. I paused my blogging and I met them in the front hall to face the music.

'You're in trouble!' sang Amanda, thrashing her hands in the air like she just didn't care. It wasn't a good look. She *should* care.

I raised my hands in defence, but of course only one came up.

'Adam, your arm!' cried my mom. 'What happened to my baby's arm?'

'I'm not a baby!'

'I'm sure there's a reasonable explanation for Adam's dismemberment,' said Dad. 'Adam?'

I was getting so used to my one-armed disability that I'd nearly forgotten.

'Oh, you know, it got sawed off by a genetically modified super-bee that was trying to turn the entire town into zombies.'

'Where's your arm now, Adam?' asked Mom.

Amanda's face fell. 'There'd better not be a limb under my pillow.'

'It's in the freezer,' I said, 'next to Dad's bac—'

I stopped myself, but the bacon was out of the bag.

Mom rolled her eyes and death-stared my dad. '*Michael.*'

Dad shot me a look.

'Sorry,' I mouthed back.

'Oh, my little boy,' said Mom, wrapping me in a hug. I put my one arm around her.

'Do you think you can patch me up?' I asked. 'It's kind of handy to have, well, two hands.'

'I'll fetch the arm,' said my dad. 'Anyone else hungry?'

'Just the arm, Michael,' said Mom.

Mom sat me down at the kitchen table with her doctor's kit and studied the hole where my arm should attach. Dad laid my dismembered arm on yesterday's sports section. It started to twitch as it thawed.

'That's the grossest thing I've ever seen,' said Amanda, backing away. 'And we're supposed to eat off that table?'

But Mom ignored her and started threading her

stitching needle. Dad held my arm up to my torso and I made the mistake of looking down. The nerve endings and bloody veins moved and twitched on their own. They were finding their matches on my body and reconnecting.

My mom was astounded. 'I've never seen anything like it.'

My dad was disgusted. 'I hope never to see anything like it again. No offence, Adam.'

'None taken, Dad.'

Mom sewed me up, tying the skin together tightly around my arm socket. I rotated my wrists and wiggled fingers to make sure the nerves were all joined up.

'Your finger,' Mom said, noticing my dislodged digit. She got to work on it, popping it back in place and sewing up the skin.

When we were little, Amanda and I had matching Cauliflower Dolls until she cut off my doll's hand for supposedly stealing one of her cookies. After she got sent to her room for invoking sharia law*, Mom

---

* How do I explain sharia law? Hmmm, that's probably what WikiPedia is for.

239

sewed the fabric hand back on. I felt a bit like that doll as Dr Mom finished her final stitching on me.

'Adam, dear,' she said. 'I know you'll tell me the full story of how you lost an arm and almost a finger when you're ready, but right now what I really need to know is: why were you on stage butchering the national anthem?'

'Thought we agreed to play to your strengths, kiddo,' Dad said, attempting jazz hands. He then looked at me with a look I couldn't quite place. It wasn't anger, but it wasn't quite rage either. 'Adam, you were very, um, ah, what's the word? Brave. You were very brave to sing like that. And we're proud of you.'

It was pride.

'You are?' Amanda and I said in unison.

'We're mostly relieved that the mob didn't lynch you,' said Mom. 'But yes, we're also very proud. It took a lot of courage to do *that* to those songs.'

'It took courage to listen to,' huffed Amanda. 'And you totally embarrassed me in front of Trigg!'

She shoved past me and pounded up the stairs. I heard her lock herself in my old room.

'She's just jealous,' Dad said, placing a new

SMOOCH baseball cap on my head. 'Almost forgot, we got you a souvenir.'

'Of what?' I asked.

'The concert, kiddo,' said Dad.

'No,' I said. 'I mean, what can she possibly she jealous of?'

'You're pretty special, Adam,' said Mom. 'I mean, you've always been special, but now you're different and special.'

'And that's making Amanda feel a bit ordinary,' said my dad.

'Thanks,' I said, taking off the cap. 'What? I don't want to get hat hair!'

Later that night, I snuggled into Lumpy Cot but was too wired to sleep. My mind raced. I worried what medical miracles (or genetic hiccups) actually lived within my undead body.

I checked on Adamini without waking him. He'd taken up residence in an open box of fabric softener sheets in the laundry room and I pulled a scented sheet over him to keep him warm.

Still in my PJs, I climbed the stairs and emerged in the back yard, hoping the blast of Croxton night air might send me to dreamland. But I wasn't the only one who couldn't sleep.

I spotted Corina perched on the roof of her house. I waved, relishing the use of my reattached arm. She gave me a subtle four-finger wiggle of a wave (no arm movement, no wrist rotation – it was the minimal effort a wave required) and then she pointed to Nesto's house. She whistled and beckoned him like a dog.

Suddenly, Nesto scaled the back fence and landed on all fours, trouncing Mom's flower garden. He wasn't in chupa-mode, but he still sprang and pounced like an animal. He was learning how to harness his powers. It would have been more impressive if it didn't mean I'd have to help Mom replant petunias in the morning. But I suppose since Mom did sew me up, it was the least I could do. Shame her flowers were at the epicentre of monster weirdness.

'Couldn't sleep either?' I asked Nesto.

'Not after today,' he said, standing upright. 'You?'

I shook my head. 'Not after what we've seen.'

Corina floated down on to the lawn and held out some Pop Rocks. 'Sleep is for the ordinary.'

'And that's not really us,' Nesto said, popping the rocks.

'No,' I said. I was a zombie back from the grave. It felt good, really good, *zomtastic*, to be back, to be with my new friends, with my fellow freaks. 'That's definitely not us.'

Acknowledgements

I have to start by thanking my wife Sidonie for her support, patience and encouragement through this long creative process. Despite all appearances, zombies do not simply rise up fully formed. This project originally started with one simple idea ('hey, let's make a zombie movie in our house') and then over time the story, characters and tone changed, evolved and morphed into this book!

I also want to thank the editorial team at Faber. I brought this book to Leah Thaxton because I knew it would tickle her funny bone, and she fell in love with Adam Meltzer. Thank you for believing in Adam! Rebecca Lee valiantly picked up the project and made it her own. Art Director Emma Eldridge created a look to make Adam Meltzer stand out in a crowd and illustrator Scott Garrett literally brought him and his friends to life on the cover.

Lastly, I want to thank you, the reader . . . especially if you're in middle school. I remember those years well, and they're not always easy. But as overwhelming as everything may seem right now, someday, not too far away, you'll look back and laugh.

Q&A with Jeff Norton

How did you get the job of writing Adam's memoirs?
A few years ago, I made a little film called *The First Zombie*, which is a documentary about an adult zombie that comes back from the grave and hopes to get his old life back. Adam found the film on the internet (it's online at: www.thefirstzombie.com) and I suppose he felt that I was sympathetic to the undead. We started emailing and he asked me to be his official biographer.

You use footnotes a lot in the book. Is this how Adam really talks?
Yes! You should see his editorial notes to me! Adam is very precise. He likes things to be just so. He claims that his guidance councillor says he has early-onset Obsessive Compulsive Disorder (OCD), but between you and me, I don't think it's all that early.

Which character are you most like?
I think Adam and I are similar in many ways, which is why we get on so well. I like to keep things neat

and tidy, but I mostly fail at that. I'd like to think I'm most like NinjaMan, Adam's comic-book hero, but I'm neither a ninja nor a crime-fighter, so our similarities end at being male.

When did you know you wanted to be an author?
I was a very reluctant reader when I was Adam's age. I didn't like books all that much and to be honest, found most books to be boring – especially compared to video games. So, the idea that I would become an author would have sounded crazy to me. But over the years, and first with the help of my school librarian, I discovered a love of great stories and turned from a reluctant reader into a lifelong one.

What's a typical working day like for an author?
I start at my writing desk every day at 7:30 in the morning. I get my best writing done in the morning. Later, if the weather is nice, I go for a run on Hampstead Heath, near where I live. I usually eat lunch at my desk and then I do editing and rewrites in the afternoon – looking at what I wrote earlier and finding ways to make it better.

How do you generate ideas for your storylines?
I usually start with imagining a world; a different place that we've never experienced before and then I imagine who would live there. The next step is to dream up what would happen to those characters. For my work, it comes from the intersection of those three elements: compelling characters, awesome stories and immersive worlds.

When you have finished writing a book, who is your first reader?
My wife, Sidonie, is the first reader of everything I write. She's amazing. She's a harsh critic but also incredibly supportive. She pushes me to make my work the very best it can possibly be.

When my boys are a bit older, I'm looking forward to sharing my work-in-progress with them too.

What ingredients, in your opinion, does a good book need?
Salty snacks! Oh, you mean what ingredients *inside* a book, not when reading a good book? I think it's different for everyone. I read a lot of non-fiction, and I really enjoy discovering a new lens through which

to view the world. That is, a way to look at things differently. For fiction, it's about character, story and world. I have to love (or loathe, but either way must feel strongly about) the characters, be hooked by the story, and get totally lost and absorbed into the world. I think the other thing that I really enjoy is when I can ask myself, 'What would I do?' If I can project myself into the role of the protagonist, imagine myself in his or her shoes, then I'm in. It's a bit like what Adam was learning about with *To Kill a Mockingbird*, putting yourself into someone else's shoes.

Do you have any tips for new writers?
I think my biggest tip would be just to write. Write consistently, and to write every day. It's a skill that takes practice. I've only been doing it for about five years and I'm still practising and getting better. In fact, the concept of dedicated practice holds for everything you want to be great at.

There's a journalist and writer called Malcolm Gladwell (he's also Canadian but, no, I don't know him) and he has a theory about mastery which he calls '10,000 hours'. He argues that it takes 10,000 hours of dedicated (consistent and focused) practice to master a skill. Any skill. For most people, 10,000 hours amounts to roughly 10 years. So when I meet writers, especially young writers, even Adam's age, I remind them that if they spend 10,000 hours on their writing starting today, they'll be masters of their craft by the time they are 22. I've noticed that most 'overnight sensations' (could be musicians, artists, writers, filmmakers, scientists, inventors) have actually been toiling away in utter obscurity for years and years before their seminal piece of work hits the scene and makes a splash; usually about ten years . . . or 10,000 hours.

What do you like to do besides write?
I work a lot because I love my work. I love willing something into existence. So, if it's not writing, it could be making a short film or making a television show.

Outside of work, I've got two young boys, so I love playing with them, teaching them things, and reading to them. Storytime is a big ritual at our house. We read a lot of books each evening. I try to stay active, especially since writing is mostly spent sitting on a hard chair. I like to go running or swimming. I also love to get to the cinema, but don't go as much as I used to. But I never miss a big superhero film!

I don't ever read fiction when I'm writing because I don't want to get another author's voice in my head, so I read non-fiction to broaden my perspective on the world or to go deeper into a subject that I already enjoy.

Oh, and I love playing with Lego!

Are you able to tell us anything about your next book?
I don't want to give too much away, but it's coming together nicely. The second book finds Adam, Corina and Nesto uncovering a grave threat on the last day of seventh grade . . .